SMALL BITES

FANTASTICAL STORIES OF FANTASY

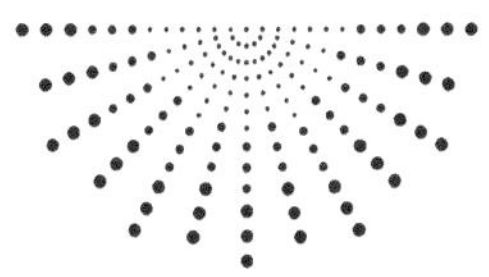

F.R. WILSON

Printed in the United States of America

First Printing, 2019

ISBN: 978-0-9995739-8-3

Detroit Ink Publishing

4444 2nd Avenue

Detroit MI 48206

https://detroitinkpublishing.com

Cover Design by Sydgrafix, Detroit MI

http://sydgrafix.com

SMALL BITES

Cast a Long Shadow

Hearts of Fire

Faces in the Fire

Planet Eden

THE LAST BEAT

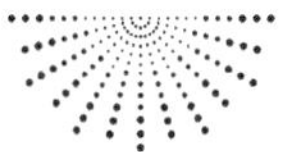

I slide into my usual booth at the back of the bar away from the pugnacious crowd up front, ignoring the condescending looks and snide comments I often got from some of the regulars. Walking that gauntlet made me feel like a balloon in a room full of pins.

The place is like any average neighborhood dive. There's a long oak bar that stretches the length of the room. High backed booths form an L-shape along the back and side wall. A dozen chunky legged tables with rib backed chairs fill up the empty space between the bar and the booths. A wall of windows with light bending glass surround the red entry door and terra cotta tiles cover the floor. The lights are kept so low it takes a couple of minutes to adjust to the dark once you come in. Which is alright because most prefer the twilight. Anonymity and a solid respect for privacy are as much in demand here as the drinks.

There are other bars, but oddly I feel most comfortable here. This bar, the Haven, is the only bar in town that caters especially to our kind of crowd. Everyone is welcomed and relatively safe here. Vampires, Witches, Fairies, Angels, Demons, Leprechauns, Nymphs; even a few humans are regulars. The crowd is diverse and relatively peaceful. The bar is considered neutral ground; a sanctuary as such. There are rivalries and most have their biases, but they manage to keep their prejudices in check. The bar never closes and is never out of whatever you may want. Everything from a draft beer to a Bloody Mary made with real blood.

"*Our kind of crowd*" I thought. I'm barely tolerated as one of the crowd. They only begrudgingly considered me one of them. After all I am, by popular consensus, a "Minor Demon. Unlike a Succubus, a Gorgon, or a Rickar. I'm even considered lower than an "imp."

I'm a Time Keeper; some call me a Time Thief or a Time Bandit. Whatever they call me, they don't like me. I prefer to be called a Horologist. It sounds more professional and not as dramatic. In fables and myths, to hype up the ghoul factor, we've been called Soul Eaters. That's a laugh to me. I've never seen a soul and the idea of eating one doesn't appeal to me at all. The fact that I only take time, the last beat of a dying heart, to other Demons, is pathetic, weak and a wasted effort. "You might as well steal their watch. At least you could pawn that for some cash," was the going joke for a while. I guess since I don't claw out their heart or consume the life of new born babies, I am a sorry excuse for a demon. No, I can't call up fire, drink a body dry, possess someone, or even compel others to my will. But, I'm more than nothing. I deserve some respect. Damn it!

Before I could whip myself into a real funk, Abby came to the table wiping her hands on a towel looped over her belt. Abby is one of the reasons, if not the main reason, I come here. She is blunt, a little crass, irresistibly friendly, and cute enough to make a Goblin blush. A perfect personality for a place like this. I like Abby even more than I am willing to admit. Her cheerful voice and familiar manner make you want to be around her. Abby wears her hair in a short bob that looks perfect with her small pointed features. She has the most hypnotic blue eyes I've ever seen. In my dreams, she's the perfect fairy princess. Her alabaster skin, apple red lips, and lean body are praise worthy. She is without a doubt, the only Vampire I have ever liked.

"You Okay, Hannibal?" Her eyes were blinking like stars.

"Sure, I'm fine," replacing my scowl with a fumbling smile.

"You just looked like you smelled a fart or stubbed your toe or something." She shrugged her shoulders. "Okay, what will you have, handsome? The usual?"

"Just a Bud Lite, please."

"No shot to back it up?"

"Maybe later."

"Let me have one of those too, Abby." Sidney requested, sliding into the seat across from me.

"Coming right up," she answered, turning and sashaying away.

I looked around. "Where's His Highness?"

"He's with the other clan leaders. Merrill wouldn't be caught dead in here. Too low-budget for him."

Sidney is the jittery type. His eyes are constantly darting about, looking over his shoulder as if he's expecting some assassin to leap out of the shadows. His short thin frame makes him look like a noodle with hair. A set of pleading brown eyes and a high impish voice do nothing to change that image. His usual uniform of all black hung on him like it was still on the hanger. The black fedora he wore looked like a dark cloud that had settled over his head. Sid always has the tense expression of someone who is holding his breath. He's a Trickster Demon and considered a Minor Demon, like me. Illusions are his power. He can make you believe you see things that aren't really there. Any mediocre Witch or Magician can do the same thing with ease. Sid compensates by aligning himself with those who have major powers.

"I'm glad you're here," he said, checking around us. "I need to talk to you. Something big is up and it's got me worried. Well, at least more worried than usual".

"What's the problem," I asked, knowing his propensity for melodrama and paranoia.

Sid is one of the few friends I have. He and I have been buddies ever since I helped him escape from a Werewolf, after he had tricked the oaf into believing he was a pack brother so he could steal gold from him. Werewolves are dumb as a stump, but you don't want to get one mad. They are deadly and powerful enemies and nothing to mess around with. After that narrow escape, he started working for Merrill, the leader of the Vamps, for protection if nothing else. Merrill may be a pompous ass, but he commands some awesome powers and is respected and feared by most everyone. He has no respect for anyone, but he's a good asset to have on your side.

"Listen, I'm serious." He leaned over the table and continued. "Merrill is down the street right now meeting with Taylor, Whitcomb, and Marble. They are planning something big. I think it has something to do with Alexander."

He stopped as Abby arrived with the beers. She smiled, winked at me, and left.

"When are you gonna make a move on her? It's obvious she's interested. She giving you all the signs."

I waved him off. I was in no mind to handle a relationship. And besides, what if she was just being nice and only wanted to be friends? I'm just an average guy and less than nobody in the Demon world. My not-so-imposing height, sleepy gray eyes, and unruly crop of thinning brown scraggly hair do not shout "catch of the day." I carry a healthy supply of what I call body armor, and a face in search of an expression. I know I'm no prize. Abby deserves more than an orphaned Minor Demon without position, power, or connections. And I deserve not to feel any more rejection than I already do.

He shrugged, shook his head, and continued.

"I know Merrell. I've worked for him for a while now and I know when he's scheming on something. If these guys are agreeing on anything, that is not a good thing. That bunch is no group of Fairy God Mothers. When they solve a problem somebody normally loses a head. I know for some of us that's not a problem, but you know what I mean. I'm telling you Hannibal there is trouble in the air." He took a long swig of beer with shaky hands causing the beer to foam out of the bottle.

"You remember how bad things got the last time there was a

big shakeup. It was years before any of us could walk the streets and feel safe. The turf wars, the killings, and the street battles. I don't want to go through that again."

I didn't want to raise the red flag, but he was right. If the leaders of the four biggest groups, the Vampires, Werewolves, Witches and Demons, were meeting and planning, despite or rather because of their natural rivalries and hate for each other, it was a big deal. There has been a truce between the major groups that has kept the peace. If that agreement was put in jeopardy because of some back room plotting, then it would be bad for everybody. Even if they were agreeing it could be bad for us peons.

"What makes you think that their meeting has something to do with Alexander?" I asked.

"Well, I heard Merrill on the phone. When he said Alexander's name, he went ballistic. He called him a bunch of names and said, 'this problem has to be put to rest.' Besides everybody knows Alexander and Merrill have no love for each other, since Alexander slapped him down when he challenged him. The next thing I know he's going to a meeting with the other clan leaders."

He stopped and downed the rest of his beer. A couple of seconds later he picked up his beer to take another swig forgetting he had already downed it.

I signaled Abby for two more.

"I thought all that was settled after Merrell took over the Vamps."

"It wasn't as neat and tidy a business as everyone thought. There were some bruised egos and serious threats made. The only way a war was avoided was because Alexander had to not only step down and relinquish all authority, but he had to accept house arrest as well. That's why he hasn't been seen for over a year."

He looked at me with eyes full of fear.

"Hannibal, I think they're going to kill him." His voice was squeaky and his breathes were short and fast. The anxiety was real.

Abby brought two more beers and I asked for two shots of Johnnie Walker Black.

Alexander had been the leader of the Vamps. He led all the covenants for over three hundred years. Legend says that he is at least 600 years old. That would make him one of the oldest of us and by far the most powerful. When you have been around that long, you gain knowledge, abilities, and powers that most can only dream of. He's learned, seen and done things most of us couldn't imagine.

"With age comes knowledge, with knowledge comes wisdom, with wisdom comes power. Power without wisdom is a danger to all life." I remember Alexander saying that in a speech once. The other clan members were jealous of his popularity and power. They banded together to take him down because no one or even two of them had the power to do it alone.

It was known that he wanted to come clean about our existence to the humans.

"No more hiding in the shadows," he said. "We have always lived in their nightmares, fables, and superstitions. Most people don't even believe we existed. We count on anonymity to conceal our presence, fearing if people knew we existed it would mean war and death."

Once when Alexander gave a speech he said, "It is time for us to come out of the closet;" a favorite phrase of the Humans. "Others have over the years gained respectability. It is time for us to stop lurking in shadows and take our rightful place, openly in society. Our time is now."

You can imagine the fire storm that created. The opposition said Humans were our prey and our chattel and we didn't need their recognition, or respect. They said it would be a step down to equate ourselves with them. Alexander argued that for the most part, few to practically none of us actually feed on Humans. Vamps switched to synthetic blood over a hundred years ago during the AIDS crisis. The Werewolves only hunt for sport, chasing wild game in cloistered sanctuaries, not the city streets. He said we had evolved and were more civilized, not the mindless monsters of history. His desire was for us to stop living in the past and join the modern world. Alexander talked about the future and how we had to look beyond what we were and see what we could become. I don't know how I felt about it. It just never seemed like an issue to me. I didn't feel like I belonged to either world, anyway.

His message swayed some, but not enough. The outcries nearly started a civil war. Things were tense for a long time. Threats of all kind were made. Demons, Werewolves, and Vamps alike went on mini-rampages. The Humans thought it was turf wars between Human gangs. If they only knew how close to being subjugated they had come. There was some behind-the-scenes negotiating, and for the good of all the clans, Alexander finally relented to the pressure and stepped down. Merrell took over and the whole matter quieted down and was forgotten.

We got our shots and two more beers. Sid downed his one after the other and said he had to go before Merrell missed him. I told him not to worry; not believing it myself. He gave me a nervous nod and left.

I sat holding, not drinking, my beer and thinking about what he had said. Abby came by a couple of times to check on me. I just smiled her away. I turned my beer up as Hiram sat down.

"How are you Hannibal? Long time since I have seen you."

"I'm good. Nice to see you, too. What brings a high roller like you to this part of town? Not much call for Angels around here, at least not your kind of Angel." I asked, half-serious and half joking.

"Oh, you know how it goes. I like to see how the other half lives and dies. Besides, I never liked the distinction between Angels and Demons. There is less difference between us than you think. After all one man's Angel is another man's…" He tilted his head and smiled.

With his wings girdled under a long black trench coat, his clean-cut college boy looks, and athletic build you would think Hiram was a military officer or a young executive. There's real power, power I envied, under that coat. Angels are some of the strongest among us. Hiram has that quiet confidence that says he's aware of that fact. His icy green eyes, sculptured cheeks, coffee-colored skin, and straight-backed posture added to his regal air. There is a hard handsomeness about him that speaks of a steely determination, but the warmth of his manner puts you at ease. Angels are a mixed bag. They are fiercely stern and yet tender and compassionate, but judgmental to a fault. I would not like to be on their naughty list.

"So how is your situation going?" He asked with raised brows.

"Let's not talk about that, okay." I said shaking my head and looking away. "It's alright. I'm dealing with it."

"Whatever you say," his hands went up in surrender. "Just let me say that you cannot ignore it; accept it my friend. It is not as bad as you think. If you look at it with an open mind you may find the upside to it. And that is the end of my pep talk."

With the seriousness on hold, we sat for a few minutes and talked about others we knew and how things had been with each other. Deciding it was time to go, I laid some money on the table, leaving a generous tip, and waved my goodbyes to Abby. Hiram and I shook hands and went our separate ways.

Walking nowhere in particular, I began thinking about Humans. We are around them every day, but they just don't see us. I don't know if that's arrogance or naivety. The majority of us are just like them. There are some of us who are just too different not to be noticed. They use illusion to mask their appearance and live unmolested. But most of us go unnoticed. We sit next to normal humans on the bus or stand in the same lines with them at the bank and the grocery store. We have jobs, families, and mort-gages. We're just like them, only they don't realize we're there.

Maybe, Alexander has a point, maybe it is time to come out of the closet. The world is different and is changing fast. After all we're already a dozen years into the 22nd century. Science has made fantastic discoveries and advances. We have all kinds of new technologies. Just about every disease has been cured, and there are gadgets for every conceivable thing. Robots clean our homes, cook our food, and run our errands. We have colonies on the

Moon and Mars, for goodness sakes. If people can accept living with robots and on other planets, surely, they can accept living next door to a Werewolf or a Mermaid.

It won't be long before we run into somebody out there from another world. *"What will that be like?"* I wondered. Maybe they'll be beings like us. A whole planet of Demons, or Fairies, a whole planet of Vamps; I shuttered. That last one didn't appeal much to me.

An alarm went off in my head. All my senses went on alert. Everything about me, my eyesight, my hearing, my sense of smell, and even my sense of taste came alive. The blood in my veins seemed to heat up and move faster. There was someone dying nearby. I am drawn to those last moments of life. It calls to me like a siren's song. I can't resist it. I'm compelled to seek it out.

Being a Horologist, I feel time, especially the end of time. I sense it. I taste it. I hear time in heart beats. The normal heart beats about three billion pulses in an average human lifetime. I hear those beats. I feel them. Every one of them. They sound a constant drum beat in the back of my mind. The rhythm, the pounding, the passing of time calms me.

Time for me is tangible and always in the forefront of my life. Time is as natural to me as flying is to a bird. I can tell when your life is winding down and you're at the end of your days. I feed on that last beat. The very last one. The period at the end of life's sentence. It gives me sustenance and nurtures me. That last tick of the clock is sweet as nectar and powerful as the first spark of a flame. A normal human can sustain me for a week. The more potent the being, the more energy I receive, the more power I gain. I don't have to be right there to feed just nearby. But, the closer the better, the more intense the experience. I never cause death or even encourage it; I just sense it's coming. It's my calling, my center. If my energy level is high enough, I can sometimes give the dying people visions to ease their way. It somehow makes the transition easier for them; for the both of us.

I could tell it was a female heart. She was not far away and very close to the end. A shiver ran down my spine. My pace quickened. I stopped a couple of blocks later in front of a poorly maintained apartment building. There were shabby curtains in most of the windows, a broken liquor bottle on the walkway, and the faint smell of urine in the entrance hall.

As I stepped through the lobby door, I could hear televisions tuned up too loud, kids crying and laughing, a couple making love, and two floors up a woman dying. I ascended the stairs and stood at her door.

When I entered her apartment it was dark, the scent of faded lilacs hung heavy in the air. The room was filled with well-worn pieces of furniture and a cold sense of solitude. There was an abundance of photographs on the tables and the walls. Pictures, old and new, in color and black and white. Photos of smiling children, Christmas gatherings, weddings, birthday parties, graduations, and all kinds of special occasions documenting a life well shared. I asked the darkness: "How can someone so proud of family, so into people, be left to die alone? How can one who lived a life full of relationships end up with only Polaroid's to witness her passing?"

She was pale and gaunt, laying under a threadbare quilt in a dim cold dingy bedroom. Her breathing was shallow and labored. I felt her heart struggling. Though the beats were weak, I could hear them resounding like a church bell on Sunday morning. A slow thunk…thunk…thunk. It was so clear. I could hear the count. Three billion, one hundred seventy-six thousand, four hundred and eighty-seven; three billion, one hundred seventy-six thousand, four hundred and eighty-eight. *"A full measure of life."* I thought. *"Such a sad and sorry end."*

Her eyes were open. She was staring at the ceiling as if she was trying to look through to heaven. I gave her a vision. I let her see the stars and the great vastness that awaited her. Brushing the loose wisps of hair back from her face I took her hand in mine.

"It won't be long now," I whispered. "The pain will be gone, and you can rest. Know that you are not alone."

She smiled. I was a little startled. She reacted as if she heard me and saw me. That wasn't supposed to be possible. During my visage I become ethereal, only my kind can see or hear me, at least until that very last beat. It seemed that lately I was losing my cover. At my last few encounters there had been a look of recognition in their eyes. It wasn't a look of fear or horror, but much like the one in this woman's eyes. A resigned acceptance.

I wondered what they saw when they looked at me. Did they see a monster? Did I represent death to them? There didn't seem to be any apprehension or fear. But it still unnerved me. In a way it seemed my presence calmed them and allowed them to let go. At that moment between life and death, when we face each other, there is a joining, a sense of oneness as we pass through each other. I guess I would never really know for sure what they felt or thought. I mean no harm and try not to cause any pain or fright, but I just didn't know.

I sat and held her hand listening to the count. Thunk..3,000,176,495. Thunk..3,000,176,496. There it was. The last beat. Thunk..3,000,176,497. I reached out with my mind and caught it like a moth in midair. We mingled and passed each other like clouds merging and then separating in the sky. Her eyes smiled with appreciation. I drank in that last beat. I gasped. The heat within me rekindled. I was sated and renewed. Time stood still. The whole universe embraced me. Time and I were one; life and death. As she moved on, I stood alone between time and space.

I looked down on this poor creature. "There Mother, you go to your reward. Your work is done here." I crossed her arms over her breast and turned to leave.

I stepped back surprised because there was Hiram standing in the doorway. His emerald eyes locked on me.

"Are you following me?" I snapped.

A smile crossed his lips as he approached me.

"No, my friend. It just seems we had similar appointments. I waited on you because I did not wish to disturb your work."

"So, I guess you saw the vile Demon doing his dirty deed," I growled.

"Hannibal, I do not judge you," he said, waving his hand.

"That is not what I witnessed anyway. I saw the gift you gave to that lonely soul. You may try to deny it, but nature cannot be denied. You take, but you give as well. Nothing is a one-way street. Everything has two sides; it is the balance of things. All creatures to their nature."

He walked closer to me.

"I figured out what was happening when you asked me those questions a while back. In that last heart beat which you consume is a reflection of the soul. The very essence of that person. You are changed by that, for good or for ill. I cannot say, but anyone would be. Only you know which. This is not a fight between good and evil, not a battle between right and wrong. This is about the essence of existence. You think you are only death. How wrong you are, my friend. You are about both life and death, the cycle of time. The way of things. After all what is life without death or death without life; one gives the other meaning. You give time it's proper role. You are an arbiter respecting and honoring both their life and their death. Hannibal, do not mistake what you do for who you are."

I stood there looking at him dumbstruck and unsure of what to say or do.

He smiled and said. "Your work is done. Now let me get to mine." He walked past me patting my shoulder. "No one should walk that last mile alone."

In a trance, reeling from his words, I walked out of the apartment and onto the streets. I moved not thinking, not aware, until I found myself sitting on a park bench miles from the apartment.

Hiram had been right. I did ask him some pointed questions months ago. I had dressed them up as a hypothetical situation and thought I had fooled him. I claimed I wanted to be sure I didn't contaminate myself with something unseemly from those dying. I could feel more and more changes happening with each heart beat I consumed. It didn't change me physically, but on another level, I wasn't the same. I didn't know what this meant, and it scared me. What was it doing to me? What was I becoming? What was I to do? The questions kept mounting and I didn't know where to find the answers.

As far back as I can remember, I've had this relationship with time. I always knew on an intimate level what time it was. If a clock was off, I knew by how much. I could tell you down to the nanosecond. I knew how old people and things were and even how old they would become. I started to know when things would die. I could hear the ticking of their internal clocks. My abilities scared my foster families to the point I learned to hide them and my thoughts. People feared me. I was never welcome anywhere for long. I started to fear being around others because I didn't know if I was the cause of their death. I learned to hide my abilities. Living with this ticking clock in my head made me feel even more separated from others than I actually was.

There never has been anyone to teach me, to let me know what all this meant. It was all a matter of instinct. It took years to give it a name. I finally found out what a Time Keeper, a Horologist, was and what they did, and that I was one. I have never met another Horologist or knew any that existed. There wasn't anyone I knew who had known one or met one. For all I knew I was the last. All I knew for sure was that I was different and alone.

The first time I fed it scared me. It was done so innocently. I was drawn to this dying man and without warning it just happened. I stood there looking at him and it came to me. I didn't know what had really happened at first. When I realized what had happened I was sick. I felt so guilty and so dirty. I hid for months. Was I a monster? Was I a killer? It took a long, long time, but slowly I came to understand and accept what I was.

"Alexander," I shouted out of the blue. He's lived longer than anyone. If anyone ever knew one like me it would be him. I could only hope he would see me and help.

After a shower, a change of clothes, and a couple of shots of scotch for courage, I rang the doorbell at Alexander's estate. A pinched-faced Vamp with a demeanor of disapproval opened the door.

"Mr. Cartwright to see Mr. Valstak, please."

After a lengthy appraisal, he invited me into the vestibule.

"Wait here." It was more an order than a request. After a few minutes, he returned and instructed me to follow him. I was led me through a lavishly decorated hall with expensive rugs, bronze candelabras, and regal portraits adorning the walls. I felt like I was going to a job interview or to a court martial. We entered a large room on the northwest side of the mansion.

"Mr. Valstak," he hesitated. "will be with you presently." He spoke with an expression that implied he smelled something undesirable. A typical Vamp attitude. I really don't like those guys. The room was a library or den with a large ornate fire place and floor to ceiling windows covered with red velvet drapes. The furniture, all antiques, was arranged in a way to promote conversation. What I could only assume were expensive artifacts were on display all around the room. Several shelves of books completely covered one wall. No museum I have ever been to could have done it better. The room said, "I am somebody." I was admiring a bronze statue of an American Indian spearing a Buffalo when the door opened.

Alexander Valstak is as impressive in person as he is in legend. He stands six-one or better, with chiseled jaw bones accented by a pencil mustache, deep set vibrant brown eyes, and a massive crown of swirling white hair. He was dressed in black pants, a green silk smoking jacket and holding a snifter of brandy. Alexander sauntered into the room and changed the atmosphere; a picture of confidence. You could feel his presence filling every square inch of the room. He belonged here. I suddenly felt as if I had made a big mistake.

"Mr. Cartwright," he said extending a hand. His voice was a rich baritone full of the steadiness earned from decades of giving orders.

I took his hand and was not surprised when I felt a cold grip that could crush rocks. "Yes, Mr. Valstak," I said, trying not to bow.

"Let us dispense with the formalities, shall we, you call me Alexander and I shall call you Hannibal. Please have a seat," he said, pointing to the sofa as he took an elaborately carved wing back chair.

"Okay," was all I could manage to say surprised that he knew my given name.

"Would you care for a drink?" I shook my head no. "A cigar perhaps." I shook again. "Alright my boy, down to business then. What can I do for you?"

"Mr. Valstak," I said. He raised his brows. "I mean, Alexander. I'm a Horologist, a Time Keeper. I was wondering if you could put me in touch with someone like me. I need answers to questions I have." I spoke quickly not allowing myself a chance to take a breath.

"Well Hannibal," he began. "Time Keepers are rather rare these days. There used to be a time when your kind were more numerous, but sadly, today your brethren are scarce. I remember when I first heard about you. I was very curious and followed your progress for some years."

"You followed me?" I asked a bit surprised.

"Oh yes, yes. I make a point of becoming personally involved with all important matters that cross my sphere of influence. And you my boy, a Time Keeper are very important. You're the first one I've encountered in many years. You really are rarer than you know. Time Keepers, Horologists, if you prefer, are like the Fates of ancient Greek myth. You may not spin like Clotho, or measure a life's length like Lachesis, or even cut the thread as Atropos did. But you tie the knot at the end of the thread to stop the unraveling of time and give that life, that time, some meaning."

He talked with hand gestures, at times I found myself looking to his hands rather than his face.

"You and your kind are Guardians of Time. You are no minor concern. You do not know how important and powerful you are. Your skills and talents have been hidden away it seems even from you." He raised his brows for emphasis.

I was not consoled by his words. "So, you don't know any others?"

"At this time, I'm afraid I don't. The last one I knew personally, tragically died, oh about 50 years ago. He was very old and very wise. It was a terrible loss."

I slumped back in disappointment.

He studied my expression.

"I think I know what you are looking for. Borgia, Pietro Borgia was his name. He and I were great friends for many years. We shared many adventures and conversations together. He was one of the finest and wisest beings I have ever known. He was older then than I am now." He gave me a sideways glance. "It's the effects of the feeding, isn't it? Changes are beginning to become noticeable to you." He nodded agreeing with himself.

A little shaken, I nodded my confession.

"Pietro spoke of this in depth. It had a profound effect on him. He found that some of the traits of the people he encountered were being imprinted on him. These things were altering his perspective and giving him unfamiliar thoughts and insights. He found that he knew and understood thing that were foreign to him before the encounter. At first, he fought it, but eventually he learned to use it and grow from it. Pieteo came to understand and accept it as a gift. A memorial, a parting gift from the dying. A way for them to leave a bit of themselves in this world, a legacy of sorts. A sort of immortality. Just as he learned that time was his calling and he developed his relationship with it. So, he did with these transferences."

"All I can tell you is that you must learn to use them Hannibal; to understand them. It can build you up in ways that will serve you greatly in the future. It's all in the way that you approach it. Pietro learned this and it made him wise and very formidable. I tell you, use what you get. Not just the energy, but the wisdom and passion that can be found in those nuggets. Hannibal you have to learn to believe in who you are not just in what you are and what you do. The one does not necessarily define the other, it can enhance it."

He paused and threw his hand up in the air. "I'm sorry my boy, I wish I could tell you more."

Disappointed by his not knowing another Horologist, I stood

to take my leave and decided that I would tell him what I had heard.

"Alexander, thank you. You have done me a service; I wish to try and repay that kindness. I think you should know I heard that the clan leaders are planning something, and it may involve you. I don't know any details but, I get the impression whatever they are planning will not be good for you. Please don 't ask me how. I know this I don't want to betray a friend's trust."

He mumbled "I didn't expect them to act so quickly." He motioned for me to sit down, I obeyed.

"Hannibal, I think that maybe we should talk some more. I have an idea that I think will aid us both. I'll order more libations and we shall collaborate." He smiled and gave me a wink.

We sat, drank tea, and talked casually for a long time just getting to know one another. He told me some of the old stories and I filled him in on some new ones. Once you get past his air of authority, he's quite a nice guy. His being a Vampire made me a little uneasy at first, but he was like Abby, genuine. A kinship began to grow between us. I started to like him as much as I admired him.

"Hannibal," he said in a tone as serious as the look in his eyes. "Do you know what special day tomorrow is?"

"No idea."

"Tomorrow is the perihelion. It is the point in Earth's orbit when it will be closest to the sun. The forces of nature will be at a powerful apex then. At this time many wonderful and horrible things can and will happen. Our friends, the clan leaders, I fear, are planning to use this special spiritual point in space and time to perform a very risky, very old ritual. They must be either very desperate or very stupid to try this. I vote for the latter."

He paused as if he had to collect his thoughts. "I must show them what a ritual can really do. This ritual, they hope, will strip me of my knowledge and powers and transfer it all to them. You see, tomorrow I will die."

I gagged and nearly spit my mouthful of tea across the room.

He smiled. "Don't be so surprised," he said. "You yourself told me that my adversaries are planning it as we speak."

"I didn't say you were going to die. How do you know that's what they're planning?" He let me go on without interrupting. "Then we've got to get you out of here. We've got to come up with a plan."

He roared a deep laugh that sounded like the rumble of an earthquake. "No, my friend. Running for life is for the young. I made my peace long ago. When you have lived as many centuries as I have you do not run from death. Death and I are old and intimate friends. I have known death as I have known life. I have wallowed in it, shied from it and even aided it. I do not fear death. For I have learned that death is just another fork in the road."

"It has been known that for some time they were planning to rid themselves of me. They want what I have. That is the only reason I have been allowed to live this long. They didn't know how to strip me of my powers. You see it's all about power and power is a strange and delicate thing. Those that don't have it, crave it, and those that have tasted it want even more. Unfortunately, our friends have never really taken the time to understand it. They will try to seize power never realizing that real power cannot be taken it must be given; freely; like rain or love."

His voice became gentle. "Hannibal, my young friend, I have had my time and more. Nothing can or should live forever. You being a Horologist should understand this better than most. I will let you in on a little truth. Things must be finite in order to be appreciated. If you have all the time in the world nothing has urgency or value. You must have the possibility of losing something in order to appreciate and care about it."

"As well, everything has its time like us and the Humans. I wanted to make an open declaration about our existence because it is time. We need the Humans. Do you know why? Because," answering his own question, "they have what we need to survive. Not as fodder or prey, but their vivacity. Their curiosity and imagination are essential elements to keep life moving forward. It is the one important quality that beings such as ourselves lack."

"Vampires, Satyrs, Angels, Werewolves, Fairies, and alike have they ever created or invented anything? No, they never have nor ever will. It is not in their nature. Humans are seekers. They are never satisfied. They constantly dream of the new, the unobtainable. They crave the adventure, the discovery. We are creatures of the past still dreaming old dreams. Humans dream of tomorrow. They dream of bigger and better and build cities in the sky. They dream of flying and end up in the stars."

"Those meddlesome indomitable children have been let loose on an incredible journey across the universe. A journey we need to join or be left behind to fade into the annals of history. A journey that you, Hannibal, need to join. Tomorrow, my boy, you will begin that journey and change the world as we know it." Alexander erupted with laughter.

We talked a while longer as he laid out a plan to me. I listened carefully feeling overwhelmed, fascinated and a bit worried. My concern and my fondness were both growing as we talked. It was almost dawn when he bid me goodnight. "I have much to do. Much to prepare," he said.

I asked as a parting shot: "You don't have to answer if you don't want to, but how old are you really? I can normally sense these things, but with you my senses are unsure."

With a half-smile he said. "Humans track their history by the wars they have fought. I have fought in many of their wars. Sometimes for glory, sometimes for fun and others because I believed in the cause. My first was the battle of Tewkesbury during the Bello Rosas." His gaze drifting to the past and he smiled. "We won. Glorious it was."

I'd have to look that up later.

After I left Alexander's, I went home to rest and think. His plan was crazy, and the implications were huge. I tried to convince him that he should escape and plan for another day, but he was determined.

"Tomorrow I am going to die." he said. "There is no escaping that fact. I could delay it for a while, but it will eventually become my reality. Our friends will see to that. This way I get to, if not control it, at least direct it. If one must dance, it is nice to be the one to choose the music."

The next night I took my prearranged place up in a large oak tree at the rear of his estate. After I was settled in, I saw Bartholomew Merrill, Sid in tow, and Agnes Whitcomb, leader of the Witches, arrive together. Not long after came Terrance Marble, leader of the Demons. Finally, Sirus Taylor, leader of the Werewolves, followed by a half dozen of his pack brothers marched into the manor.

Committed and hunkered down, I was still troubled with worries. Alexander had been very convincing and showed no signs of doubts. I fell victim to his optimism, but I still held some reservations. They were in there plotting his death and who knows what else. I wasn't sure he could do all he claimed, and I began to wonder if this would go terribly wrong for the both of us. There was no doubt that he was in there taunting and irritating his advisories, making matters worse; if they could get worse. That was his way. Alexander was either incredibly brave or just plain crazy.

The Wolf pack began patrolling the grounds. Knowing they live more by smell than vision, I had sprayed the area around the tree base with a skunk extract. The scent would mask my own. It wouldn't scare them away, but it would cause them to give the area a wide berth. Sitting on my perch, I watched them do their job and return to the house. I rappelled to the ground and took my position behind the manor ready to play my part. Alexander told me he would be able to communicate with me and I would see what he saw. He said we would be as one. I didn't quite understand how he was going to make this happen. Despite my misgivings on some level I believed and trusted him.

There was no moon or stars. The skies were thick with clouds swollen with the promise of rain. Dampness hung heavy in the air. It was cool and refreshing like wet kisses. The musty smell of the earth, the rhythmic chirping of the crickets, the electric charge in the air that danced on my skin. Something about this night seemed alive and vibrant. The world felt ready for a happening.

I felt something like a headache coming on and my vision was beginning to blur. Then just as fast everything became calm and came into focus. I was seeing through Alexander's eyes. I was, I mean Alexander was, in a dark room lit by dozens of candles. Four figures stood before him. The first I noticed was Merrill. He was to his left staring grim faced. His stout frame loomed ominously like a mountain of dirt. Merrill's large bulging eyes made his face look like he was about to explode.

Agnes stood next to Merrill looking like a Swedish pin-up model gone Goth. Her shockingly pale skin and set of bodacious breasts that demanded their own attention distinguished her from your ordinary witch. She was reading from an old tome on a dais before her, using elaborate hand gestures to punctuate her words.

A hairy Sirus was next to her sneering like a junkyard dog. His image seemed to shift from man to beast and back again. Terrance was the last of the quartet. His tail was coiled about his feet and his horns were peeking from under his hat. The Demon leader stood nervously licking his lips and as if he was waiting on the call to dinner.

Alexander looked down and I could see he was seated with his arms bound to a chair by chains. The chair was surrounded by a circle of glowing stones. Runes and symbols were drawn on the floor and walls in what looked like blood.

I could faintly hear what I though was Alexander in the distance. I called his name, "Alexander."

Agnes's head snapped up from the tome she was reading. "What is it?" Merrill asked.

"I thought I heard another." She closed her eyes, tilted her head and listened. "There are so many spirits here," she said returning to her chant.

"Let's get on with it," Sirus grumbled.

"We can't rush this. If we want the rewards we seek, this must be done in the right way. This is a very delicate business. One mistake and we could lose everything," Merrill insisted.

"Let's just make sure that we all get what has been promised to us," Terrance added. "I'd hate for this to end up with disappointing results. The repercussions would be tragic, at least for some," his tail whipping up to a point to emphasize his words.

"I would be cautious with my threats, Demon." Merrill shot back.

"Look at all of you. The sorriest excuse for leadership I've ever seen. Standing there arguing like bratty children fighting over toys. Don't worry Marble, no one will get your share of the stolen spoils because I assure you there will be nothing to divide. And if there were spoils, do you really thing Merrill would share it with any of you like a good little Vampire?" Alexander laughed at his captors.

"What does he mean by that?" Sirus asked.

"Don't listen to him. We have a deal. He's just trying to create dissent." Merrill barked. He started to approach Alexander with fury in his eyes.

"Do not break the circle." Agnes shouted. "You must not compromise the circle."

He stopped and spat at Alexander, baring his fangs. His words were like steam escaping from a whistling tea pot. "You are going to die. I will have all your knowledge and power, old fool. I will wipe your name from the world and make sure everyone knows what a pathetic being you really were."

"We," Marble said smiling. "We are going to have his powers."

"Yeah," the Werewolf added, growling and showing a mouth of sharp canines.

Merrill turned and gave them a look that could melt iron.

"Pathetic." Alexander roared with defiant laughter. "Simply pathetic."

"It is upon us!" Agnes yelled. "Everyone join. We must link. Cautiously, the quartet formed a half circle.

"*In Omnibus Potentiis Quae Possunt Fieri!*" Agnes shouted. Again. "*In Omnibus Potentiis Quae Possunt Fieri!*"

The candles began to flicker, and the rocks began to glow white hot. There was a rumbling as if the ground was going to open up. Shadows danced about as a wind began to build.

"Get ready!" I heard in my head. Alexander was mumbling in

the background. I just couldn't make out what he was saying. He chanted very fast in a language I had never heard before. Alexander threw his head back and let out a scream of words like a police siren. "Let my will be done!"

My head wrenched back as well as I was feeling and doing the same thing. "Let my will be done!" I repeated. The world went black and I was standing in a void. I was nowhere. There was only darkness as far as I could see. A black nothing, above me, underneath me and all around me.. Then Alexander was there. He smiled and offered me his hand. I took it.

A stream of energy coursed between us. We joined as we flowed into each other's orbit, becoming one. I could hear and feel the beat of time unlike anything I had known before. It was more a boom than a thunk. The count was enormous. BOOM. Twenty-five billion, three hundred eighty-seven million, one hundred ninety-nine thousand, seven hundred and forty-three; BOOM. Twenty-five billion, three hundred eighty-seven five million, one hundred ninety-nine thousand, seven hundred and forty-four.

"Take it," he said. "It's all for you."

I opened my mind and became a vessel. It came to me. I felt the rush. It was like capturing the caboose of a runaway train. Like taking a seat on the sun. I was filled to the point of bursting. It consumed me and washed over everything. I was drowning in it. It was ecstasy. It was pain. I had never felt anything like it before. It was coming so fast and intense; it became too much. I fell to my knees sinking into the wet grass, cupping my head. I doubled over, gasping for air, and trying to remain conscious. It was an avalanche of time, flowing like blood from an open wound. It was an ocean of time, drowning me. My heart was beating so fast I thought it would burst from my chest. Time was alive. Time was life. I was life. I was time.

The deluge suffocated me, eclipsed me. My breath stuck in my throat. I trembled as my mind turned in on itself. The past, the present, and the future rushed at me all at once. I was time and time was everything.

"Run!" Alexander shouted. "Run now!" I watched as he smiled and began fading away.

The screams and howls that came from the house brought me out of my trance. It sounded like a war was under way. I rose from my knees and on wobbly legs, I ran. I raced through the park that abutted the back of the estate. Tears were mixed with the falling rain as I took off in a blind panic. I ran down streets, between cars, around buildings, through parking lots, into traffic, down alleys and empty lots.

I just ran never looking back, never slowing. My mind was in a fever and my legs were on auto pilot. I was unfocused and unstoppable. Strange images ran through my mind and stranger feelings were surging through my body. Things unknown to me raged inside me claiming my sanity. I felt the tug of time pull me forward and backward. I don't know if I was running from something or to something. I just ran. My tears flowed like a broken faucet. I ran until I collapsed in a muddy ditch. I laid there exhausted and confused sobbing like a lost child.

I woke in my bed not knowing how I got there and still wearing my shoes and clothes form that night. They were ripped and caked with dry mud. "Alexander," I whispered burying my face in my pillow and cried again. "He's dead." I knew it. I felt it. I laid there for hours trying to come to terms with what had happened.

Three days passed before I could make myself leave the bed. I was in a state of total apathy. My world had been turned upside down. I felt disjointed as if I no longer belonged to the world I knew. My mind didn't feel like my own. My thoughts were still jumbled and unclear. It was as if I had been born this morning and everything was strange and new. I had to get out of here.

As I walked the streets, my head began to clear. There was no doubt things were different. Something hung in the distance just out of reach. There was something new in play. Even time felt different. It wasn't just minutes or years or heart beats. It was something new. A new power. I felt it as sure as I felt the breeze on my face. There was a new sense to everything. My senses weren't just different. I was different, more complete. I wasn't frightened. I felt a belonging. I didn't feel I was just part of something, instead, I felt that that something was a part of me.

I ended up at the Haven. The bar was busier than usual. I uncharacteristically walked in, slowly surveying the room. There was a tangible tension in the air. Inquisitive eyes and bowed heads turned up as I passed. I was pleasantly amused.

Sid was sitting at our booth. I sat down across from him. He didn't look up. He slumped in his seat, both hands hugging a beer bottle.

"Sid, what's wrong? "

He just stared at me.

"Hey buddy, come on, what's up? What has Merrill done now?"

"That's not funny. You know Merrell is dead," he muttered.

"Dead. I didn't know. I've been out of the loop for a few days." I said innocently.

"Well yeah, Merrill is dead. It happened at Alexander's estate three nights ago. They were in one of their secret powwows and who knows what happened. We had to break down the door to get to them. Merrill looked like a deflated balloon. Hannibal, I've never seen anything like it." He paused and took a deep breath.

"They were all messed up. Taylor has gone mad and is in a steel collar and chains so he won't claw out his eyes or rip out his throat. Marble's in a state of deep shock. He doesn't talk, or eat, or nothing. He just lays there with this look of terror on his face. By all accounts, he's as good as dead." He sighed and shook his head.

"Poor Whitcomb, she's been mindwiped or something. She can't remember anything. Not even who she is. She spends all day crying and screaming."

"The clans have gone to hell with no one to lead them and to top it off, Alexander's missing. So, you want to know what's wrong. Oh, nothing in particular. How about you?" He said sarcastically ending with a pout.

"That must have been the screaming I heard before I ran." I thought.

"Alexander, what did you do to them? How did you do it? And what did you do to me?" I finally asked. "What happened?"

"Nobody knows for sure. Like I said, they were locked in that room and something just went horribly wrong. I told you there was trouble brewing. They were in there messing with some powerful mojo. When we looked in it was like hell had come to visit."

"Don't worry, my friend. They only got what they asked for just not the way they expected it," I said. I didn't know where that came from, but it felt right. Sid sat up and stared at me as if I had declared myself king of the universe.

Abby strutted up to the booth. "Hey, Hannibal, the usual?"

I grabbed her hand and pulled her into the seat next to me. She came willingly.

"Not today," I said. "Not today or ever again. How about you and me go out and change the world? I think there's a future out there calling our names."

"Are you asking me on a date, or is this an invitation to a revolution?" she asked blushing.

"Both," I shot back. "One at a time or together if you like."

She rose giggling and in a soft voice said. "I get off at seven." She left without taking my order only looking back and smiling.

"Whoa, where did that come from?" Sid asked. "That was smooth. What's got into you?"

I smiled shrugged my shoulders and said, "It's just a matter of time."

2

MILLICENT AND MARTHA

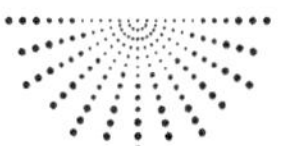

"You're telling me sir, that we are destitute?" Martha asked, pouring tea into the rose-patterned porcelain cup. Her eyes riveted on her task. Carefully scrutinizing what was being said, as well as what was not.

"Basically, that is the situation, madam. Unfortunately, your investments went, how do they say, belly up." Theodore Hatfield answered, lounging in the plush Victorian chair like a well-fed cat. "Don't despair, I am certain we can come to some accommodation?" His tone shifted from a funeral dirge to the ching-ching of a cash register as his eyes crept around the room assessing the well-kept antique furnishings. Smoothing one hand along the fine upholstery, he stroked his substantial chins with the other. "You are not without options. I could have my appraisers here…tomorrow… to take a look at some of your finer possessions." Hatfield angled forward, offering up a tobacco stained gapped toothed smile.

"As well, there is this lovely manor." His wattle swayed as he took in the full height of the twelve-foot ceilings with their ornate molding and scrolling plaster work. "After all, two," he took a deep breath, "mature women in such a large dwelling must be terribly taxing." His smile stretched from ear to ear like a Halloween pumpkin.

Martha regarded the well-fed man with polite disdain. He made her think of a grave robber scanning the obituaries for fresh prospects. She stiffened her back, smoothed her well quaffed chignon, and offered him a saucer of biscuits. Looking at Mr. Hatfield and then beyond him, a new-found glint appeared in her eyes. She smiled, picked up a pair of sterling silver thongs, and asked in the most gentile voice possible. "One lump or two?"

"One should be sufficient," he smirked.

Martha nodded. With her free hand, she tugged on her pearl earring. "One it is."

With a mighty two-handed swing, Millicent brought the full weight of the large wooden mallet down on his head. "Crack," the sound was much the same as the noise the porcelain cup made when it crashed to the ground, only louder. Theodore Hatfield wobbled to his feet, took two steps, and collapsed into the middle of the room.

Martha looked at Millicent. In an exasperated voice, she exclaimed. "Dear, your attire. After all it is tea time and we do," she glanced at the convulsing body, "have a guest."

Millicent dropped the mallet, cinched her bathrobe around her neck, and dropped into the vacated chair.

"I'm sorry dear, there simply wasn't time. I was desperately entangled with Mr. Chesney." She leaned forward and whispered. "The poor dear had a most inconsiderate hairball."

Martha raised a disapproving brow and passed Millicent a cup of tea and sipped her own. She tilted slightly looking at the quivering man.

"That is quite a lump rising on his head." The movement stopped and he laid still. "I guess he at least knew the density of his skull. One lump was sufficient."

Millicent sat down her tea cup and took a biscuit. "Yes," she agreed, reenacting her swing with a smile. "At least he was reliable on that matter." Pointing at the crimson flow seeping from Mr.

Hatfield's cranium, she mused, "That's going to leave a most troubling stain."

"Indeed," Martha agreed with a sigh; lamenting the damage to the Persian rug.

"What shall we do with him, dear?" Millicent asked between nibbles.

Martha dabbed the corners of her mouth with a lace napkin. "I suppose we'll have to do as father used to say whenever a fox would get into the hen house."

"Goodness, what was that?" Millicent asked snapping off a bit of biscuit.

"If you can't have chicken, there's always fox." Martha smiled and poured more tea.

3

JACKED

"What am I supposed to do about that?" Mayor Mott asked, pointing out the window at the crowd from his perch behind the drapes.

"Save the magic. Stop the killings," shouted the crowd between boos and hisses as they marched outside the mayor's office. Each time the chanting reached a fever pitch, random streaks of stray magic dust rocketed upward and exploded into bright displays of red and white. Each day the crowd grew and so did their anger.

"They have the right to protest," Constable Wrenfield mused, stroking his red goatee. "Besides, they have something to be upset about."

"You have to put an end to these killings. Things must calm down." Mott wiped sweat from his brow. "Since only magical folks have been killed they are sure that the culprit is a human. The humans are sure it's one of the magical folk and are angry they're being accused. This is a recipe for disaster. Those old hags, the Vaglen Sisters," he said, pointing at two of the marchers, "threatened to hex me and my whole family if I didn't quickly do something about this situation."

"I'm afraid that's easier said than done. Whoever or whatever is behind these killings has been very clever at hiding their tracks. Most anyone could have done in the gnomes. They're magical creatures, but their powers are minimal, and they have little physical strength. And yet, to kill the griffin and a witch as formidable as Selena, we're talking about someone with substantial powers at their control."

"See here, Wrenfield. It's taken years to develop this peace between the humans and the magical folks. All that's now in jeopardy. If this situation isn't resolved soon, things could revert to the chaos of the past. Maybe even an all-out war. I won't let our town, my town, be torn to pieces. I've worked too hard to establish this peace. Since Jack slew the giant we've been a happy kingdom. Even the king has been pleased. I will not lose that." Mott slammed his fat fist onto the desk. His wrinkled brow creased with even deeper furrows. Sweat glistened on his reddening face like wax on old wood. He wiped away the agitation.

"Tell me you've found something useful. Do you have any suspects?"

The diminutive man closed one eye as if focusing on something in the distance. He combed his goatee. Wiggling his fingers after each down stroke as if he were flicking away crumbs.

"Things about these crimes strikes me as odd. The methods, the necessary powers, and the selection of victims. The only thing these crimes have in common is that the victims are all magical folks."

"It had to be one of their own. It takes magic to overcome magic."

"One does not have to be magical to wield magic," Wrenfield corrected him. He stroked his goatee again, first with one hand, and then the other.

"The gnomes were rooted out of their hovels and pummeled to death. Their homes were destroyed. The griffin, a wild creature of the forest, was ripped in two and its eyes gouged out. That took considerable physical strength. Selena had things of value; gold, gems, and potions. But, nothing was taken. Her home was smashed and torn apart. Selena's body was crushed under a marble slab; again, considerable strength. There is the question of a connection. What factors connects them? There aren't any serious rivalries going on within the magical community." Resting on the thought, he shook if off and began to pace and talking more to himself than the mayor.

"These can't be random acts. There must be a goal, a pattern, a motive. What do these individuals have to do with each other? What is the connection?"

Wrenfield's pacing increased with the depth of his thoughts.

"Smashing, stomping and tearing are physical acts done in a state of extreme anger. You could call it rage." He stopped and twisted his whiskers. His tiny eyes brightened as his thoughts became clearer to him.

"Someone wanted to inflict pain on them." He looked up at the mayor. "Someone wanted revenge."

"Revenge for what?

"I don't know…not yet. But, I'm sure of it." Wrenfield punched the air. "Once we figure out who, then we will understand why."

"I still believe it's one of their own. That Troll under the Appletree Bridge and the Griffin hated each other. What about those Vaglen sisters, there was a well-known rivalry between them and Selena," Mott mumbled.

Wrenfield raised a brow at the mayor.

"There are all manner of spells, charms and amulets, any number of things that carry powerful magic and anyone with the right knowledge can use them."

"Yes," the mayor replied. "But, where could one acquire such a thing? Only from the magical folks." He said answering his own question.

"The magical folks hold their secrets very close." The sound of anxious feet and a hurried knock at the door interrupted him. "Come in, blast it."

A panting and dishelved Manni Clooq rushed in, nearly

plowing down the smaller man. "Constable, you've got to come. It's happened again." He wheezed out between breaths.

* * *

"Every bone in his body has been broken." Doctor Tindelspin stated, shaking his head. "I can't imagine how this could happen unless he was crushed under a great weight or fell from a great height."

Wrenfield looked around the secluded glen. There were no mountains or large rock formations, only a pasture of grass and wild flowers. He knelt over the prone figure of Asweld Kanon.

"Can you tell if this death is connected to the other?"

The doctor hunched his shoulders. "No way to tell you that." He frowned and departed.

"This complicates things. Now we have a human death. The list of possibilities has grown." Wrenfield mused. "What's this?" He asked, finding something under the dead man's body. It was a disk as large as a dinner plate. He held it up to the light. "It's a disc of some kind. Maybe a charm. But, I don't sense any magic."

"It's strange. Why are those four holes in the middle?" asked Clooq.

"I don't know. None that I've ever seen. But, in an odd way it seems very familiar. I'll study it closer later." He placed the disk in his satchel.

"Who was the last one to see him alive?"

"I don't know. Maybe Jack. He's Kanon's best friend."

Wrenfield and Clooq approached the house on the hill Jack bought for his mother with the gold he'd taken from the giant's castle. Before Wrenfield could knock, Jack flung open the door.

"What do you want," he hissed.

"Jack, Asweld Kanon is dead," the constable said. Jack looked around with a wildness in his eyes but did not react to the news.

"Can we come in? I was hoping you could answer some questions that may help us find who did this."

"I haven't the time. I'm very busy," Jack growled, blocking their path. "I don't know anything. So go away."

"Is everything alright, Jack?" he asked peering around him. "What's that sound? Is someone playing music?"

Jack stepped outside closing the door behind him. "I can't help you. Go away. I'm very busy."

Jack's ill-fitting shirt caught Wrenfield's attention. The observant constable froze. He touched the disc in his bag. A connection in his mind began to form. "When was the last time you saw Asweld, Jack?"

"I haven't seen him in weeks." he snapped. "I don't know anything. Now go away." Jack entered the house and slammed the door.

"That was strange. What's wrong with him?" Clooq asked.

The erudite constable pulled at his goatee. "I don't know, but something is not right. We need a new insight. I have an errand for you, Clooq. Go and ask the Vaglen sisters to make themselves available. Their assistance may be needed. I have to go see Belva. Only she can give me the answers I need."

"Belva? Do you really think that's a good idea? That witch can't be trusted. She is dangerous."

"You let me worry about Belva."

Wrenfield approached the entrance of the cave. Gingerly he edged forward, his head snapping from left to right looking for any sign of movement.

A voice sounded in the darkness. "Come, Wrenfield. There is no need for caution. We are old friends."

Wrenfield moved deeper into the cave. The crystals in the walls and ceiling began to glow. A stark white light filled the chamber, blinding the dwarf and causing him to raise an arm to shield his eyes.

Belva sat upon a throne of ivory and gold. Blue crystals sparkled around her head like stars. Her gaze slowly sweeping from one stunningly beautiful picture to another. One with green eyes and flaming red hair, to one with gray eyes and black raven hair, to one with brown hair and piercing hazel eyes. Each picture more alluring than the last, and each with a smile more menacing than the last. She settled on the one he knew best; stark white hair, piercing brown eyes, and pouty lips that begged to be kissed.

"Belva," Wrenfield said. "The years have been good to you. You are as lovely as ever."

"You always did have a sweet tongue, my little red dwarf," Belva laughed. "You have come to Belva for answers."

"In matters of magic, there is no one greater."

"Such praise. Your need must be great."

"Let us be honest. You know why I am here."

Belva shrugged. "What will you give Belva? A blood offering for my garden? A year of life? Perhaps," Belva exploded in a puff of smoke and reappeared behind him. She whispered in his ear. "Perhaps, an ear, an eye." She drew in a breath, "Your heart?" She added "again," and walked away with a laugh.

Wrenfield swallowed. "The choice is yours. You have the gift of sight. You see beyond the obvious. What do you know of these killings?"

"First, the payment." Belva returned to the constable and plucked a strand of his red hair. "A promise that you will come when called." She looped the hair and secured it in the cuff of gown.

Wrenfield nodded.

"Have you asked yourself why you have not heard the thundering footsteps of the giant's wife, angry at the death of her husband? Have you wondered why she did not hurl boulders from the sky in revenge for his death? Who lays buried at the foot of the beanstalk? What other magic did the giant have in his treasure room? These are the questions you should ask," Belva said.

"The Griffin and Selena could see through magic. We can't have knowing eyes see our real selves, can we? And Jack, well, let's just say, Jack is more than he's ever been. Answer these questions and you will know what needs to be known." Belva turned her back to him.

"Go now. You have much to do." She disappeared and the cave went dark.

. . .

XXX

"ARE YOU ABSOLUTELY SURE ABOUT THIS?" Mayor Mott asked, eyeing the twin Vaglen Sisters, Velda and Vega. Wrenfield nodded, wringing his hands. Mott leaned down and whispered. "What are they doing here?" The sisters squinted disapproving eyes at the mayor. Mott snapped to attention and return a half-hearted smile.

"After my encounter with Belva, I am certain we will need the sisters' assistance."

The mayor bristled. "Belva, she scares me more than those two. Can you really trust her?"

Wrenfield ignored him and approached the Vaglen Sisters. "Alright ladies, take your places, please. Remember, wait until I give the signal. If he becomes aware of what we're doing, he may have time to counter your magic. You must be quick with your attack before he has time to change. I don't know what manner of magic he may have with him so we must be very careful." The sisters nodded as one and retreated to opposite corners of the room.

"He's coming," said Clooq, entering the room moment ahead of a violent knock on the door.

"Enter!" Mott yelled.

The door opened and two soldiers pushed Jack in. His eyes were ablaze with anger. "What's the meaning of this? How dare you send soldiers to bring me here?"

Clooq slipped out of the door without Jack noticing.

"We asked you here to help you, Jack." Mott said calmly.

"Help me? Who said I need help? I just want to be left alone." He waved his fist. "You'll be sorry for this." Jack moved to leave the room.

Wrenfield stepped in front of him blocking his retreat.

"Move little man or…"

"Or what?" Wrenfield countered taunting him. "You'll stomp me to death? Rip me into shreds and gouge out my eyes? Maybe, you'll crush me under a stone slab?"

"You crazy little dwarf. What are you talking about?" Jack spit out, his eyes nervously gauging the others.

"I think you do. Jack. Or should I call you Clotus!"

Jack laughed. "You're crazy! Clotus is dead. I killed him when I cut down the bean stalk."

"That's what you wanted us to believe, but through magic you've survived and have taken over Jack! Haven't you Clotus?"

"You're mad! Stop calling me that!"

"Am I? Then you won't mind if we dig up that hole and see who really fell from that bean stalk, will you?"

Jack shook with anger. "You meddlesome little dwarf!" he shouted, lunging forward. Wrenfield ducked under his arms.

"Now, ladies!" he shouted.

The Vaglen sisters sprang out of their hiding places. Velda cast a binding spell, while at the same time Vega cast a sleeping spell. The magic collided over Jack's head and exploded in a blinding light. Jack froze, arm outstretched, a hateful scowl plastered on his lips.

"Thank you, ladies. That was excellent work." Wrenfield said, brushing himself off and fluffing his goatee. The sisters smiled and curtsied in unison. "Let's just make sure he stays this way." Wrenfield approached Jack and examined the immobile man, especially his shirt. He removed the disc from his satchel and held it next to one of the buttons. "This," he held up the disc. "was found under Kanon's body. At the time, I did not realize what it was. I thought it was a charm of some kind, when in fact it's a button."

"A button," everyone in the room said at once.

"Yes. A button off the shirt of a giant. When we went to question Jack, I noticed that this disc was an exact match to the buttons on his shirt. The very one he is wearing." He pointed to the spot on the shirt where the button was missing." Kanon must have grabbed at it as he fought for his life. When we were at Jack's house I heard music; harp music. Everyone knows Jack keeps the harp locked away because it will pluck violently at its own strings making horrible sounds. But this was pleasant music. The harp is friendly only to Clotus." He nodded. He began to pace back and forth.

"When Belva confirmed my suspicions, the pieces started to come together.?

"This is not Jack?" the mayor asked.

"Yes and no, mayor. This is Jack, but also Clotus through some diabolical magic that has taken control of him. Our best guess is that Jack is a prisoner in his mind and Clotus is in control of his body. It seems he is able to be Jack or Clotus, whenever he wants."

"Magic can do this?" the mayor asked.

The Vaglen sisters stepped forward, hands on their hips and their long black hair waving like angry serpents. "Magic can do anything." They chanted in unison sneering at the mayor. He retreated behind the constable.

Wrenfield smiled and fingered his goatee. "After leaving Jack's place I went to see Belva. I sent Clooq to get the sisters just in case they were needed." He bowed to them and they returned the attention with an un-witch-like giggle.

"She told me the griffin has extraordinary sight. It can see through the veil of magic. Clotus had to get rid of him or he might reveal his deception. Likewise with Selena and Kanon. They must have realized that Jack was not really Jack and so they had to be eliminated."

The door opened, and in came Clooq and Jacks' mother, Dariana. "She was there just like you said constable. He had her chained in the kitchen."

Wrenfield nodded. "I thought, at least, I hoped he would have kept her alive to cook and clean for him."

Dariana cautiously approached her son. "Jack, are you in there, son. My poor boy." She stroked his face. Turning to the others. "How could this have happened?"

Wrenfield took her hands and lead her to a settee and sat beside her. "When Clotus was an infant he was left on the gnomes' doorstep. They took him in not knowing who or what he was. They loved and cared for him, but he kept growing and growing until he out grew them. A giant, even a giant child cannot live in a gnomes' little underground hovel. They had to force him to leave. He has hated them ever since. When Jack started making his forays up the beanstalk and returning with treasures from Clotus' castle, he started planning his revenge. Not only on Jack, but on the gnomes as well. With the help of a magical talismans he has been able to fool us all. Walking among us, killing at will."

"But a giant made the hole we filled in. Who died when Jack cut down the bean stalk?" Clooq asked.

"I would say," Wrenfield wondered aloud. "It was Clotus's wife who fell. He already had control of Jack. The hole was so deep we couldn't tell who was in it. We took Jack's word for it and filled in the hole thinking we were burying Clotus." Parting his goatee like a curtain, he continued.

"Clotus chopped down the beanstalk, killing her as punishment for her trying to escape. As well, it provided great cover for him. No one would suspect him because we all thought he was dead."

"What are we to do with him?" Mott asked.

"The sisters have agreed to work on a way to remove Clotus from Jack." Wrenfield looked moon-eyed at Dariana. "We'll get him back. I promise."

"We will," said the sisters in unison, marching past the mayor, making sure to step on his toes.

The room flashed with a light that blinded everyone. When their sight returned, Belva was standing next to Jack, examining the amulet that hung around his neck.

Everyone gasped and took a step back.

Wrenfield arose from the settee and approached her. "Belva, what are you doing here?"

She swept back her purple hair and stared at him with piercing hazel eyes. "I have come to offer my aid." There was a laugh in her voice.

"We appreciate your kindness, but…"

"You want your Jack back and Belva is the only one who can make that happen." She looked to the Vaglen sisters. "No insult… sisters." She hissed. The sister crossed their arms and looked away.

"But, there is a dark element to this magic. You wouldn't want there to be any mistakes, would you?"

The constable looked to the sister who gave him a shrug of surrender. He looked to Dariana; her eyes full of tears. Mayor Mott and Clooq stood trembling unable to take their eyes off of Belva. "Can you release Jack and rid us of Clotus?"

Belva smiled and snapped her fingers.

Wrenfield closed his eyes and swallowed. "What do you require?"

Belva laughed again. "Fear not." She leaned to his ear and whispered.

"Lover," as she made eye contact with Dariana. "I only wish this small trinket." She pulled the amulet from inside Jack's shirt.

The mayor chimed in. "But that's dangerous magic."

Belva silenced him with a look.

"Agreed," Wrenfield said.

Belva pulled a wand from her sleeve, waved it, and a black cloud engulfed Jack.

Dariana whispered, "Jack."

Wrenfield moved to her side and took her hand.

The smoke began to spin faster and faster, becoming darker and finally disappearing into the amulet. When the last of the smoke vanished, Belva snatched the amulet from Jack's neck. He crumpled and collapsed onto the floor.

Dariana and Wrenfield ran to him. "Jack, Jack, my boy are you alright?" she cried.

Jack coughed and smiled up at her.

"He will be fine and annoying as ever." Belva said. She turned to leave, but pivoted back. Retrieving the strand of hair from her cuff, she let it float to the ground as it disappeared in a puff of smoke. Wrenfield felt first a kiss to his cheek then a slap.

"Debt paid. When next we meet…" She paused. "Just pray we don't." Belva raised her arms and disappeared in a flash.

"I don't think it was a good idea to give up something so powerful so easily," the mayor said.

"Could you have stopped her from taking it?" Wrenfield asked. Mott mumbled and stepped back.

"I don't know how to repay you for what you've done for me and my boy." Dariana said blushing at Wrenfield.

Wrenfield stroked his goatee and smiled. "We'll think of something."

4

DESIGNED TO IMPRESS

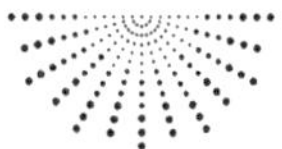

"I love your bag; it's very unusual," the woman extended her hand.

Stella stepped to the side, avoiding the contact. The hand was left hanging like an unwanted vine on a fence post.

"Thank you," she reluctantly replied, never turning to face the woman.

Her enthusiasm unabated, the woman continued. "The material is so unusual. It must be an exotic skin. What kind? Ostrich, python, caiman?"

Stella increased her stride, outpacing the woman. She muttered a response as she passed out of range.

The woman froze. Dumbfounded she stared at her companion and asked. "Did she say Walter?"

5

CRAZY DEAD

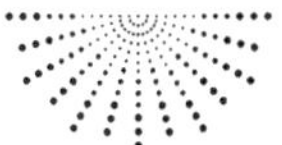

"What's going on?" Phil merged into the group.

"He's at it again." Mary pointed.

Phil sighed. "What is it this time?"

"He's exercising," added Michelle.

"Exercising what? And for what?" Phil asked.

"Beats me," shrugged Fred. "You know Eric. He's always doing something… different."

They watched in bemused disbelief as Eric finished his set of jumping jacks and started running in place. He dropped to the ground and began doing pushups. The group lumbered as a single body forward.

"Eric, what the hell are you doing?" asked Phil, his head wobbling on his slanted neck.

"Twenty, twenty-one," counted Eric lowering and lifting his body.

"Eric!" Phil shouted.

"Twenty-five," Eric rose to face the group. "Sorry. I heard you. I didn't want to lose my count." He cocked a smile of rotting teeth. "Hey guys. What's up?"

"What the hell are you doing?" Phil demanded.

Eric patted his stomach. "I'm getting in shape. You know, toning up."

"Toning up?" Phil crunched his face into a ball as if the words were painful to hear. "Why? What good do you think that will do?"

"Just because our situation has changed doesn't mean we should let ourselves go. We've got to stay in shape. You know like they say, if you don't use it you lose it."

"Its official," said Mar,y slapping her thigh sending a flurry of dried skin flakes into the air. "He's lost it."

"Eric," Phil massaged his temple. "Does the word zombie mean anything to you? I know it can be difficult to deal with or maybe you just forgot for a moment but trust me on this one. You're a zombie. You're dead." He swept out his arm in an arch.

"We're all dead. You know, not alive. No heartbeat, no breathing; dead. For God's sakes, man, have you gone crazy as well?" He looked at Eric as if he was a red traffic light waiting to turn green. "Being that we're dead and with the zombie thing and all trying to stay in shape seems a little pointless."

"Yeah," agreed Fred. "He's not only dead. He's dead and crazy."

"Dead and crazy. Or is it crazy and dead?" Asked Michelle. "Whatever it is I hope that it isn't contagious."

The group turned and stared at her. "Well, it's just that we already have enough on our plate."

"This is even better than his idea to pickle ourselves to get through the winter," Fred laughed.

"Or his idea to wrap ourselves up like mummies and wait for them to find a cure," added Michelle.

"A cure for being dead?" laughed Mary. They all hacked and coughed their way through a fit of laughter that sounded like an out-of-tune orchestra.

"Okay, okay. Forgive me for being an optimist. I have not forgotten that we are zombies. I just realized some things," Eric offered in his defense.

"Some things like what? Asked Phil.

"Just think about it. We eat, but don't gain weight. Where does it go?"

"What do you mean where does it go? That's a dumb question." said Michelle.

"No, it's not." Eric insisted, crossing his arms over his chest and looking smug.

"It went where food always goes. You know," said Phil. Everyone nodded in agreement.

"Okay then. Why don't we get fat? How come nothing came out?"

"Ugh, that's gross," squealed Mary.

"It may be gross," said Eric. "But it's something to think about."

"What does that have to do with exercising?" Asked Phil.

"What I figured out was what we take in doesn't just sustain us, it revitalizes us. Not like food did when we were alive. We don't grow, but the food is used in a different way. We metabolize everything. That's why there isn't any waste. It keeps us from decaying. From turning into dust and blowing away. We don't gain weight. We don't poop. We renew and keep going. It's like pouring water on a dry sponge." Eric cracked the bones in his neck.

"Have you ever really thought about what the term 'the living dead' really means?" He raised his brow. "Huh?"

"That's crazy talk," said Phil. "We're dead, and no amount of anything is going to change that."

"Of course not, but what we need to do is maximize what we take in and let it do its thing. If you don't believe me feel this." He held out his arm. "Go ahead Mary, touch it."

Mary poked at him with two dry graying fingers snapping off her nails in the process. "Hey, he's springy. Not all dried out."

Michelle jabbed a cautious finger into his side. "She's right. He feels like sponge cake instead of a piece of cardboard."

"He's still dead," groaned Fred.

"Of course, I am. Maybe you should try it Fred. It might help with that eye thing you've got going."

Fred reached up and pushed his hanging eye ball back into its socket.

"Will it stop my hair from falling out?" asked Michelle, reaching up and yanking out a clump of hair that looked like straw.

Eric shrugged his shoulders. "I don't know, maybe. It couldn't hurt."

"This is crazy," said Phil. "You're dead man. Face it. You're a zombie. You'll walk around eating whatever you can catch until you rot and fall apart. It's what we do."

"I think there's more to it than that," Eric replied.

"You think it could do something about this?" asked Fred, holding up his mangled left arm.

"I don't think you can grow another hand Fred. But, it might fix that bum leg you're dragging around."

"I sure would like to do something about this peeling skin," Mary said, rolling off a six-inch swatch from her bony leg.

"What do you think?" Michelle asked the others. "Maybe there's something to this."

"You're all crazy!" Phil yelled spitting out a tooth. "I guess next you'll be telling us we can fly. I'll have nothing to do with this. Just except it, you're dead." Phil gave the group a squinting eyed reproach and limped away.

The next morning under the canopy of an oak tree, Phil watched the group, led by Eric, creak and pop dry bones through a routine of calisthenics. "Crazy dead," he mumbled.

6

HOMESTEAD

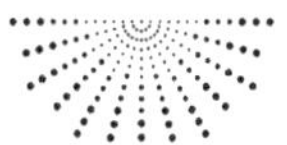

"Varied climates, fertile land, abundant water, lush vegetation, plenty of resources, and in an optimal location. No neighbors for light years. This place is a paradise. What else could you ask for?" the real estate agent asked.

"What about the pestilence problem?" the buyer asked. "The place is horribly infested."

"Don't worry about that. Our extermination team will cleanse away anything you don't want here. Just worry about what you want to name it. How about something ethereal. Or something to honor your mate or maybe one of the kids. Earth doesn't do it justice."

ALEX'S MOTHER

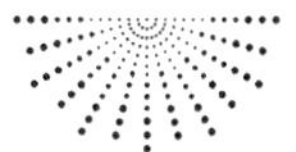

Alex wouldn't be still. Red faced and insolent, he stomped about, jumping and waving his arms like streamers. Saliva and mucus covered the lower half of his face with a beard that looked like a jelly fish.

"I won't go," he shouted, wheezing and whining with the exasperation of an overworked engine. "No matter what you do."

His mother's vacant eyes stared at him. Her pupils were full of disdain and revulsion. Straining to find a morsel of sincerity and affection in her voice, she whispered, "Alex, dear." The words were strained and hollow as they squeezed their way through her clenched teeth.

"It's been a week since you…" she paused and rethought her words. "…since the incident," she continued. "This is how things are done. If you fight it, you will only make it harder on everyone."

Whipping his head from side to side he yelled. "I don't care." His face was awash in tears. "I won't go." He kicked out, striking her calf. She winced and sucked in a scream, her eyes becoming daggers. "You can't make me." Alex taunted, falling down and rolling on the floor. Alex's mother lowered herself into a chair, pressed her lips into a tight thin slit and played the disinterested audience; stewing in her silent ire. Alex raged on like a fire devouring dry kindling.

Alex's bereaved father drove his wife to the chapel unaware of the vengeful apparition that hounded her. Alex stood behind his mother in the back seat of the car, yanking her hair, kicking her seat and shouting in her ear. She watched him through the rear-view mirror with eyes as cold and lifeless as lumps of coal. Anger was brewing in her heart.

Emerging from the vehicle, Alex's mother scanned the gathered crowd. A practiced misery in her eyes. Hesitant smiles and sympathetic nods greeted her well-played attempt at grief. Any public display of emotions was held back by propriety and an absence of the necessary ability.

During the ceremony, Alex pinched her, stamped on her feet and hammered her with blows. His wailing voice tickled the ears of the other mothers present and produced a general feeling of discomfort, but it did not elicit any reaction from his own mother.

At the conclusion of the service, Alex's mother lobbed a hand full of soil onto the powder blue box. She dabbed at her eyes and lowered her veil. Everyone mistook her audible sigh for a mother's tearful whimper. Not the sigh of relief that it really was. Nor did they notice the faint smile beneath her veil as she exited the cemetery.

8

BETTER WITH SUGAR COOKIES...

"Candy, what's wrong? You look befuddled. Have you been chugging the eggnog again?"

"Of course, not," she said, snapping to attention like a wooden soldier. "I'm just a little beside myself at the moment." She held her head and batted her eyes as if she were awakening from a deep sleep.

"Let's sit down. The break area is usually empty this time of day. We'll have some hot chocolate and you can tell me what's going on."

Leaning on Jumper's arm and tiptoeing, as if the floor was made of egg shells, Candy allowed herself to be led to the employees' break area. Jumper bought hot chocolates with miniature marshmallows and a half dozen sugar cookies, because as everyone knows, everything is better with sugar cookies. After a few sips of chocolate and a couple of cookies, the blush returned to Candy's cheeks. Her mood improved and she was again the rosy-cheeked elf Jumper had always known.

"Okay, Candy, tell me what's upset you so."

She drew back like a frightened child. "I don't think I can talk about this."

"All come on. This is me, your old friend, Jumper. You can tell me anything," he said with a gapped tooth smile.

She hesitated, looked around to make sure no one else was listening and began. Her voice, at first, just a whisper, but grew louder as her story went on.

"As Head Letter Reader in the Department of Requests, it's one of my duties to select a few letters to present to the boss. It lets him get to know the requestors, you know, the children, so they aren't just nameless faces. It's the personal touch. The fact that it's good PR, doesn't hurt either." She snapped off a bit of cookie and continue talking. "I carefully review the 'Naughty and Nice List' to see who's in and who's out, then I make my selections."

"Letters normally start with a greeting about how much they love him and how good they've been all year. Then they list their good deeds. "I kept my room clean. I didn't fight with my sister. I fed and walked the dog every day. I don't get upset when Grandpa calls me by my brother's name." You know the usual. Finally, we get to the request. "I want a doll. I need a bicycle. I'd like a puppy. I can't live without an Xbox." It's what you expect. Some are exhaustive lists of whatever they're hawking on the television. Those usually come from the ones who barely made the list. They ask for a lot hoping they'll get something before they're misdeeds are discovered, and they get booted off the Nice List."

"Then there are the returned requestors. The ones who were just reinstated after they reformed their behavior and passed the review process. Their requests are considered on a probationary basis. Joy handles those. She's very good at character assessments," Candy beamed with pride. "I trained her myself."

"Some letters are tragic and even heart-wrenching. The ones who want their daddy to come home, their mommy to stop drinking, or to help their grandfather get that prosthetic leg; things better directed to a social worker or the police department. Blizzard handles those. He's sympathetic, but firm. I wish I had more like him. He doesn't let sentimentality override his better judgement."

"Now and then we get an unusual letter. Last year a boy wanted a gift certificate for an exorcism for his sister. Or the girl who asked for a genuine shrunken human head." She bristled and took a moment to brush cookie crumbs from her sweater.

"I opened one such letter this morning. It caught my attention because it came in a black envelope, which stood out because they are normally bright red, green, and white. There was no return address. It was simply addressed to "Claus." I opened the envelope. I removed the letter, which was black also and…and…" Her complexion became as pale as snow. Her curls went limp and sagged like wet noodles. Faint puff of air came out of her trembling lips.

"Breathe, Candy, breathe." Jumper said, waving a sugar cookie under her nose. "What in the world is it, Candy? What about a child's letter could upset you so much?"

Finally catching her breath, Candy composed herself and continued. "To my horror, the vile thing was written in what looked like blood. I dropped it to the floor. I was mortified." She pressed her palm to her chest.

"I would have kicked it into the fireplace except my reaction drew the attention of all the other elves in the department. With their eyes glued on me, I had to recover quickly." She raised her small pointed nose skyward.

"I take my job very seriously. As head of the department, I must set a proper example of professionalism. I can't allow morale or discipline to waver, especially when we are so close to the big day."

"I picked up the contemptuous thing and read it. I was surprised. It was actually a very good letter. The writer was polite. The punctuation was flawless. He was clear and concise. His requests were not unreasonable. I began to think I may have over reacted and improperly judge the situation. It was who the letter was from that finally undid me."

"Who was it?" Jumper asked, caught up in the mystery and spraying crumbs as he anxiously nibbled on his cookie.

Her voice dropped back to a whisper. "It came from his son." She raised her eyebrows and tilted her head down.

"Who?" Jumper asked. "Whose son?"

"Him," she mouthed the word and looked down again.

"Who is him?"

"Him." She said more vigorously through clenched teeth, adding a downward pointing finger along with the eye movement.

"Him?" Repeated Jumper, looking from side to side for a clue. His eyes opened like a budding flower as the realization came to him. "Oh dear, him. His son."

She nodded. Her eyes wide open as a wooden doll.

"What are you going to do?" he asked reaching for another cookie.

"I don't know." She slumped in her chair. "Nothing like this has ever happened before. The implications are profound. We get request from all kinds, all over the world. How do I classify this one? Just another child and nothing else? We've never made any distinctions before. But, would this set a precedence? Create a new standard? I can't just ignore it. Do I pass this one to the boss and let him decide? Does his request get granted? Or does he get a lump of coal?"

Candy leaned on the table. "Can we hold it against him because of who his father is? After all, what has he done? He's just a child, isn't he?"

Jumper answered with a shrug. "I can't imagine ignoring a child. But, then again this could start an avalanche? Are we going to start getting requests from every…I don't know…every whatever in the universe?"

Candy pinched the bridge of her nose. "What if we decide to turn him down? Will his father feel we've insulted his son? If so, what might he do?" She bit her lip. "Jumper, what would you do?" Her eyes pleading for an answer.

Jumper leaned back in his chair, shaking his head. "I don't know. We don't have these kinds of problems in the sleigh shop. The biggest issue we ever had was when the boss had that near miss with the 747. We installed hazard lights…" He clapped his hands, "…problem solved. Other than adding padding to the seat and changing reindeer poop bags we are problem free. This one is way over my head." He gave her an apologetic smile.

"This is a nightmare. I'm just two seasons away from retirement. This could ruin my career if I make the wrong decision. This is worse than the time the workers went on strike over losing their nap times and we had to import toys from China."

"Yeah," Jumper palmed his last bite of cookie. "Quality plummeted. We lost our Q-1 rating and got audited for the next three years. Things weren't very merry around here for a long time."

"I just don't know, Jumper." she sighed. "After all his name isn't on the Naughty List. I checked. So, he's entitled, isn't he?"

"Is he really on the Nice List?"

"Technically, no." She admitted. "He's really not on any list I could find. His name just…never came up."

"I'm glad I don't have to decide this. I not sure I could." Jumper downed his chocolate and chewed on the remaining marshmallows. His eyes twinkled mischievously. He moved in a little closer.

"Candy, what did he ask for?"

Her back stiffened. She shook her head and pressed her lips together like a child refusing to take medicine. "I can't tell you that. There's a privacy policy that individual request cannot be revealed. Even in this instance, I have to adhere to the rules."

"I understand," he sighed with obvious disappointment. "Well, whatever you're going to do you don't have much time to do it. The big night is less than a week away."

"I know," she breathed, exasperated. "I was on my way to the legal department to talk to Cinnamon. I need advice. I have to know what my options and obligations are." She cradled her head in her hands and groaned. "Jumper, you have to promise to keep this to yourself. I've already said more than I should have."

"Don't worry, Candy. Your secret is safe with me."

"I've got to go," she grabbed the last sugar cookie and raced down the hall.

That year a new stop was added to the route. In anticipation,

he left out a glass of milk and a plate of treats, because as
everyone knows, everything is better with sugar cookies.

9

NEITHER SHEATH NOR SWORD

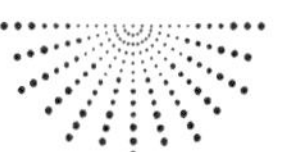

The chamber guard read the guest card and looked up. "My lady," he stuttered trying to mask his surprise.

"Madame Ambassador," she corrected him, and moved to the arch of the doorway. She stood; hands crossed over her ample bosom, allowing the door to frame her as if she was a Renaissance masterpiece.

"Ambassador Esperelda Adona DeQuallan of the…the Marrepan Republic," the chamber guard sang out. A hush fell over the room. All eyes turned to the door. All held their collective breaths. Not a hint of movement could be detected underneath her high-collared frock as she sauntered into the room like a swan gliding over calm water. The skin-tight bodice of embroidered black silk and lace hugged her sinewy frame so tight it was hard to believe she was breathing. The voluminous purple satin skirt of her gown hid the stilettos that clicked, clicked on the marble tile like knives stabbing the silence. A hint of orchids and jasmine filled the air causing each person to breathe her in as she passed by.

A thick braided crown of midnight black hair sat above her

chiseled cheek bones. Scandalous blood red lips and an imprudent Byrundium pug nose announced her claim to royal heritage. A single piercing gray eye focused ahead like a raptor locked in on its prey. The other eye was covered by a diamond encrusted black velvet patch. Her expression was both haughty and stoic. She looked neither right nor left, acknowledging only the path ahead.

Esperelda stopped several steps before the throne and ever so slightly bowed, spreading her arms wide like an egret landing. Never easing her steely gaze nor relaxing her high held chin. "It is a pleasure to see you again, my liege. It has been too long." Her casual greeting was cloaked with irreverence.

As stunned by her appearance as the others, King Gergori cleared his throat and nodded an acknowledgement. Struggling to find his voice he finally said. "You as well, Esperelda..." he cleared his throat again. "...dear cousin." His fingers danced busily on the arm of his throne.

King Gergori Matanous DeQuallan was a young man with a hook nose, vapid deep blue eyes, and a growing paunch. Esperelda saw only the same truculent, pimply-faced youth she had grown up knowing. She was still unimpressed.

His eyes evaluated her with an uneasy caution. "You have altered greatly since our last encounter. If you were not announced, I would not have known you."

Gritting her teeth, she said. "When last we met, I was not my own. I dare say, court intrigues overshadowed a cloistered child." He shifted uncomfortably.

"I am intrigued," he cupped his chin, concealing a smirk. "You are the Ambassador?" He asked. She nodded.

"But, you are Byrundium. Marrepan is the enemy."

"Only if you wish them to be, your highness."

Gergori relaxed and chuckled until the solemn expression on her face gave him pause. "Surely, you jest?" He asked tilting his head.

"I am not known for my comedy, highness. I have been accused of being somewhat witty, at times, but never truly humorous." The cynicism in her reply chilled the air. "Especially," she added. "when the topic is of such a dire nature." She smiled, revealing a perfect set of alabaster teeth. Her eyes were as wide as a cat sizing up an unsuspecting canary as she said, "I have come to discuss the succession of all hostiles." She leaned in and spoke the words with purposeful clearness.

"To end the war." The gallery erupted in a cacophony of mumbles and whispered comments.

"What could a woman," he waved a dismissive hand, "even a noble woman, possibly know of war? It is not a topic for tea parties, sewing circles, or in birthing rooms." A muffled guffaw filled the gallery.

Esperalda moved two steps forward. The click of her heels silenced the room. "What is war, but treachery, betrayal and violence? As you know, I am intimately acquainted with all three." The words caused Gergori's chuckle to end abruptly.

"I have come to offer an end to 75 years of bloody animosity between the continents. No doubt you wish to end it. Surely you will not continue as your father and his father before him did?" She paused as if waiting for an answer, but continued before he could speak.

"Or would you prefer to try the Quaddrel, once again?" The gasp from the gallery sounded like the wind rushing out of a tunnel.

Many crossed themselves and clasped their hands in supplication. Others, in fearful piety, closed their eyes and offering prayer. The mention of the dark arts was not only frowned upon, but thought to invite misfortune. The public speaking of such things was unheard of. To imply that the king was involved in such practices was sacrilegious at best and treasonous at worse. An accusation that could not be ignored.

The king fumbled nervously, looking around the room. He stood and shouted. "Clear the hall. Everyone out!" Eyeing his ministers, he added, "All!" Esperelda almost giggled.

As the royals, courtiers, ministers, and sycophants fled out of the chamber, she wandered about the room casually examining its treasures. Removing a glove, revealing long black lacquered nails, she tinkled the crystal prisms on a pair of harp-shaped candelabras. Sliding her hand down a 6-foot-tall vase, she took in the cool smoothness of the porcelain. Respectfully, she cupped the chin on the bust of Byrundium's most decorated general, her favorite uncle, Polotus DeQuallan. A wide berth was given to the display of knives and swords as she unconsciously brought her hand to the eye patch.

"What did you hope to accomplish by this, Essy," said the king, breaking her contemplation.

Esperelda looked around the empty room as if looking for the girl whose name he spoke. "A name from the past. No one has called me Essy since I was a child. Long before…" her voice trailed off. The thought, like smoke, lost to the wind. Whirling around to face him, a moment of mutual repugnance passed between them. A long edgy few seconds shadowed in dark remembrances.

"Why did you not request a private audience if you sought retribution for the past? You would have been more effective out of the public eyes and ears. Impugning my name will not strengthen your cause. Is this some Marrepan plot meant to weaken my authority? If you seek to undermine me, your efforts are wasted." His bluster grew. "Showing up after all these years as the Ambassador of the enemy, my dear cousin, is not clever.

"A private audience? The thought never occurred to me." She brought a hand to her throat. "Closed doors are so insidious, cloaked in deception. I prefer to live unfettered." She shrugged her shoulders. "As for being an agent of the enemy. I assure you, I am no such thing."

Gregori eyed her warily. "How could you, a member of the royal Byrundium bloodline, turn on your own people and become a Merrepan puppet?" The impatience of one not used to opposition began to creep over him. "Tell me, what is this solution you spoke of? What is this, no doubt, duplicitous offer of peace?"

"Magic," she answered matter of factly.

Gregori laughed, snorting like a piglet. "My dear cousin, magic is dead. Dead and gone. I have magicians and wizards and beyond a few party tricks to entertain children and the feeble minded, they are useless. Magic died years ago, it is all used up, Essy. There is no more magic. You waste my time with lifeless dreams."

Meeting his eyes with the authority of a tutor correcting a prideful student, Esperelda spoke. "It is true that the arrogant conjurors of the past and their single-minded overlords, on all sides, drained away magic in their feeble attempts to win dominance over each other. That is why the skies are locked in a perpetual night. Why the land is scorched and barren and the seas are a sickening miasma of sloshing muck." The disgust in her voice etched itself on her face. "Not aware enough to understand the extent of the devastation they wrought, they built metal monsters to continue their killing and destruction…"

The king dismissively interrupted her diatribe. "Yes, yes. You are repeating history we all know."

"But," she said stabbing the air with a nail that gleamed like the polished steel of a tiny dagger. "Thank the Goddess, all magic is not lost. She withdrew its essence and locked it away from the reach of the undeserving. Saving it for a saner time. Magic," she smirked, "my dear cousin, still exists."

Esperelda walked over to the empty throne and smoothed her hand over the velvet upholstery. She turned to him and smiled. "It lives like a smoldering ember hidden under layers of spent ash. All it needs is a little encouragement to be rekindled. A puff of air." She exhaled slowly. "A breath." Esperelda stepped away and spoke over her shoulder. "It is truly possible to reignite that flame and return the world to what it once was."

"The Goddess is a myth. Her stories are a relic of the past."

Esperelda spun on her heels and stomped her foot. "There is more in the world than your…" she hesitated, took a breath and added, "than your dreams can imagine."

"I don't know about that," he bragged. "My dreams can imagine many things. But, let's play along. How do you know this? What knowledge, what insights have you gained?"

Esperelda began pacing a circle around him causing him to track her like a child spellbound by a butterfly.

"I was in the eastern province recovering." She tapped a nail on her eye patch. His pale cheeks flushed as he diverted his eyes. She answered his reaction with a smirk. Her voice grew deeper and more entrancing.

"I was safely away from the machinations of the court. Being a young naïve female, I was considered of no consequence and so I was permitted to be forgotten and live. In my exile, I met a most unusual clan of people. They took in a traumatized disillusioned one-eyed orphaned waif." She paused savoring a warm recollection.

"They tended my body and then my mind. I was introduced to the Goddess. Not just the idea, but the Goddess herself." She raised her hands, palms up in supplication, "All praise be to her. She opened the world to me. A world of limitless possibilities. In her grace, I learned many things. Her knowledge, wisdom and power vastly outshine the speculations in your libraries of systems and numbers. Under her tender personal tutelage, I learned to see and to understand."

"That does not explain your present situation."

"After much instruction and mentoring by the goddess, I was directed to approach King Darsion of Sardos, and to initiate talks with King Valpan of Marrepan. They, like you, did not, at first, see or understand what was being offered them. But, after some gentle persuasion, they have come to see the light. Now Sardos and Marrepan are at peace."

"Is this your plan?" He yelled. "To gather our enemies against us?"

"Calm yourself, cousin. The Goddess does not seek war. She wishes to extend this offer of peace and prosperity to Byrundium as well. That has always been the intention."

Gergori's breath was shallow and quick. Nearly groveling, a hint of desperation entered his voice. "How can this be done? What is the price for this peace?"

"Simply to understand and accept."

"Understand what? Accept what?"

She stopped pacing and gave him the paralyzing stare of a spider eyeing a fly in its web. "To understand the need for repentance, salvation and redemption. To understand how a deplorable whelp could maim his innocent bride to be. Why her father, mother, and brother were unmercifully disfigured and killed. Why the world has been thoughtlessly savaged by greedy miscreants. And," her cat's smile returned, "to accept what must be done about it."

Gregori eyes blazed with rage. He produced a jeweled dagger. "I knew you sought to usurp me. I should have slit your throat as well as take that eye." He attempted to advance on her. "My legs. I can't move my legs." A mixture of disbelief and fear gripped him. "Witch," he screamed. "You have hexed me." Gregori looked down and saw the thin circle of powder that surrounded him. He began screaming. "Guards, guards. Where are the guards?"

"They cannot hear you, cousin. Nothing you do or say can leave that circle. We are alone just as we were 15 years ago, when you changed my world forever."

"You cannot blame me for what happened," he stuttered. "I was young. I was under the control of my father and his necromancer, Laxus. It was Laxus' idea to perform the Quaddrel. He needed the body parts for his magic. He and father are the villains. I was but a pawn. I was in fear for my life."

In vain he strained to free himself, his eyes darting about wildly "My guilt has been my punishment. I have suffered greatly." Gregori mouthed wordlessly trying to construct excuses. His explanations turned into bargaining pleas.

"Please cousin, how can I make amends? What is it you want? Anything. I can give you lands, titles, treasure! You can be my queen and rule at my side as it was supposed to be!" His voice growing louder and shriller with each word.

"Your judgment is not mine. I am neither the sheath nor the sword. It is the Goddess who demands an equaling of the past."

She rippled her fingers. "A small remittance for the returning of the flame of magic."

Esperelda smoothed the soil over the last of the four small graves that contained a heart, a liver, a tongue, and a diamond encrusted black eye patch. Taking a moment for remembrance. She dabbed away the tears that fell from her gray eye. The blue eye did not weep.

10

BLOWBACK

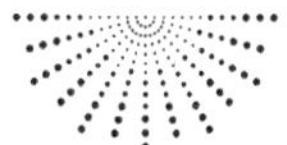

Curtis stared down the barrel of the gun at Tony's pained expression. Their eyes locked in an embrace of sadness and fear.

Aaron stepped between them, spreading his arms, causing his coat to fall from his shoulders.

"Choose," he shouted in a spray of spittle. "Us or this?" he said, pointing at Tony while also dismissing him with a wave of his hand. Half a dozen figures flanking him voiced their support with hoots and fist pumps. He paused. "Or accept the consequences."

The threat hung in the air like a putrid odor. Aaron's smile slid across the words like butter on a steaming baked potato.

"Shoot!" he demanded through clenched teeth taking a step back.

Curtis felt an angry chill grip his spine.

"Do it," Tony whispered, staring at Aaron. He was as casual and defiant as a pugnacious five-year- old facing down a dare. Thrusting out his chest, he turned to Curtis.

"It wasn't meant to be." He whispered the words as they died on his lips. His eyes shined with unshed tears.

Curtis's heart pounded in his ears. His fingers ached to release his grip, but fear pressed his palms tighter to the trigger. He couldn't remember how the gun got there. Only that no matter how much he wanted to throw it away something told him he couldn't. Curtis eased his hold. He closed his eyes. The gun angled down.

"No," Tony shouted reaching out toward him.

"Look at me." Curtis head snapped up, so did the gun. Tony stretched to his full height. His face a block of granite. "You have to." The words were cold and definite. He bit his lip.

"I want you to. If you don't, we both lose."

Curtis shook his head. He parted his lips. No words came out, only weak puffs of air; almost a cry. His eyes fogged over. A flood of emotions threatened to burst out like a sudden summer squall. Curtis looked from Tony, to the gun, to Aaron and back again.

Aaron hissed. "Where do you belong, little brother?"

Tony and Aaron shared the irreverent stare of old rivals. Their eyes full of the anger and resentment earned from a long-fought war.

Tony placed his left hand on his chest and flagged his finger. A gold band refracted the dim light from the lone street light. With a broken smile, he nodded.

Curtis clenched his teeth. "Bang!" the shot was a thunder clash. Blood gushed from the hole through Tony's hand. He closed his eyes and crumbled to the ground. Curtis's lip quivered. He never looked down. Tears covered his cheeks.

Aaron stood over the body gloating. "Bang!" A shock of disbelief on his face. He fell. The hole in his head spewed blood and brains.

Curtis dropped the gun to the ground and walked away clutching the gold band on the chain around his neck.

11

THE LADY DECLINES

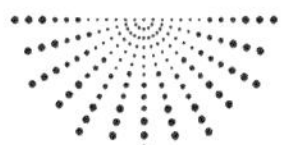

A year to the day, the boat thudded against the rocky shore. A wooden plank lowered. The ferry man descended and walked to the edge of the wall of mist. Bowing, he extended an emaciated hand. Out of the opaque barrier, a slender arm appeared, laying smudged fingers into his control. He winced at the sight of bruises around the wrist. With loving gentleness, he escorted the Fairy Queen, Allouous, out of her prison of fog.

Tattered layers of silk streamed behind her like waves of fading light. Tousled curls of midnight black cascaded down her back. A high held chin and impertinent nose gave no agency to her condition. Without words, she glided to the bow and placed herself like a masthead of stone at the helm. She stared into the distance. Her face was a dignified mask of resolve.

The ferry man pushed from the shore, careful not to jostle his precious cargo. With long full strokes, he propelled the craft. The pole produced no sound as it made contact with the rancid water. His respectful, yet rapacious eyes stole admiring glances at his ethereal passenger.

The haunting caws of a flock of crows pierced the deafening silence. A dark shroud cloaked the sky like a funeral veil. Cool dampness hung on the air as if it was wet linen. Twisted trees armed with razor sharp thorns guarded the banks resembling a battalion of weathered old soldiers. The broken remnants of battle littered the landscape; broken swords, shattered shields, and crippled lances. The ravished landscape stretched out in all directions fading into a blur of fog. It was a land devoid of life. A dank graveyard in monument to the death of a dream.

On the opposite shore, the walkway lowered. Allouous disembarked and entered a waiting carriage. The ferryman stood vigil watching the brougham melt into the mist.

Allouous remained cloistered until the transport halted at the castle entrance. She walked straight to the throne room, never acknowledging the familiar surroundings. Had she looked around her, she would have seen the destruction done by those who searched for the secret only she possessed.

For the first time she found an object of interest. Like the first star in the night sky, her eyes were drawn to the sparkling diadem. The golden headdress atop the Troll queen's head shimmered in her eyes like a thousand suns.

The Troll queen rose from the stolen throne, her expression full of disdain. She reached up toward the too-small crown that tilted mockingly on her head. Their gazes collided. Time lost its moorings. The Troll queen rushed forward, her face flushed and her eyes full of anticipation.

Allouous met her eye to eye. A single sway of her head delivered a thunderous, "no." The Troll queen bristled with anger. A violent thrust of her arm, pointed Allouous back the way she had come. The Lady again let her eyes rise to covet the jewel. She slowly released her gaze, pivoted, and returned to the waiting coach.

The ferry man solemnly transported her from one shore to the other. Before releasing his hand, she ever so softly squeezed his gaunt weathered fingers. Without look or word she merged back into her captivity of mist. The ferry man returned to his craft clutching the hand to his heart.

12

STOOL PIGEON

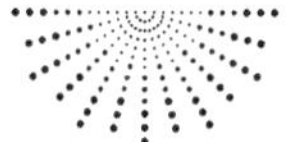

The plane sped away. Marcus looked out the window at the wild flapping arms and legs of Sid as he plummeted toward the ground. "Huh," he said to himself. "I always thought pigeons could fly."

13

THE OTHER PART

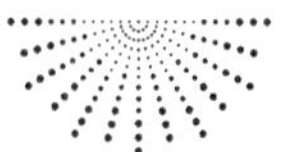

Cupping the knife in his palm, Maximus closed his fingers around the sharpened steel and opened a gash in his hand. Blood leaked from his clenched fist like sap from a freshly severed branch. A slick pool of red formed on the stone altar. He reached inside his tunic and retrieved a locket of ribbon bound hair. After pressing it to his cheek he placed it in the frothing liquid. It soaked in the warm fluid until the black tresses took on the red hue of his blood. With the scarlet brush, he wrote J-E-B-E-L-L-A, on the stone. "It won't be long, my love," he whispered.

The red moon reached its aperture as the magic forces he summoned gathered and pushed against the natural world. Winds began to gust and swirled about like a gathering storm. Maximus covered the altar with a red silk cloth tattooed in the dust of crushed gems with runes and symbols. Maximus repeated over and over the chants from a weathered leather tome. Sweat covered his body as the intensity of his chants grew. His chants became prayers. Prayers so deeply felt within him that he wept the words.

Tears were not easy for Maximus. His soldier's heart was hardened and forged by strict training and many brutal battles. He believed a man showed his strength by a force of arms, like his warrior father taught him. Tears were for children and old women; a sign of weakness and an admission of powerlessness. Then she happened, the beautiful Jebella. She softened his heart and gave him new eyes to see the world differently. Her love and tenderness showed him there was more than one kind of strength; more than one kind of power. She gave him a reason other than battle to live.

This night he cried as never before, even more than when he heard the news Jebella was dead; executed because she had chosen him. That day his heart had stopped beating. That day he felt it seize up in his chest and shrink to something so hard and cold that if you opened his chest there would be a lump of stone where his heart should be. The heartbreak was so deep he had to stop feeling anything or die from the pain of it.

From that day on nothing mattered. Even then he cried not only because he'd lost her, but because he wasn't there to protect her. Because someone who had given him so much should suffer so much for him. He cried because he couldn't say goodbye. He cried because he could do nothing else. Now he cried for her return. This was his last chance to be with the only thing that had ever meant anything to him.

Maximus saw the cloth begin to rise and fall as if the silk was breathing. Slowly it began to fill and take shape. Inch by inch, something was there. Was it her? Had the gods granted his hear's' desire? Or had he conjured something from the depths of the netherworld? Some evil to taunt and vex him with his failure? Had his magic failed him as he had failed her? Could this torment, this guilt, finally come to an end?

Maximus knelt at the side of the covered shape and pulled back the silk. It was Jebella. Just as he remembered her, just as he had dreamt of her; untouched by the years. The touch of his hand caused her chest to rise, she breathed in and out. He watched as her smooth young breast rose and fell with life. Her skin began to glow and regain its honey-colored luster. He caressed her small hand as her fingers warmed to his touch. "She lives," he gasped, amazed and relieved at the same time. The storm of pain he'd been lost in for years began to clear. The lump of stone in his chest ignited. His heart began to beat again.

Jebella's almond-grey eyes fluttered open and she whispered, "Maximus."

"Yes, my love," he said, covering her with kisses. "It is I. Jebella my dearest, I have missed you so." His head fell upon her neck and he thanked every God and every deity that had ever existed; laughing and sobbing at the same time.

Through her haze she asked "Where are we? How am I here?"

"I will explain it all. You must rest now. You have been through so much. There is time. Just rest. Regain your strength." Maximus moved Jebella over to a bench.

Jebella closed her eyes and drifted off to sleep. Maximus stared at the prone figure. He stroked her hair, her limbs, and her face; touching them to reassure himself that she was real. Once again something mattered.

Jebella's sleep became fitful. She tossed and squirmed, calling out several times as if she were in danger. Maximus worried over her, wiping sweat from her brow and re-covering her each time she kicked off the cloth. After several hours, she awoke, wanting food and drink. They ate and drank; Maximus never taking his eyes from her for a second. The joy in his heart radiated like sunshine.

"I cannot remember ever being so famished or so thirsty," she said.

"It has been a long time," he admitted timidly approaching the subject.

"What do you mean, Maximus? Do you have something to tell me?"

"What is your last memory?"

"My mind is cloudy. Nothing is clear," she said, shaking her head as if she had just risen from a pool of water. "I almost feel as if all of me isn't here. It's as if there is a part of me missing." She shook away the thought.

"I remember Alturust. He was jealous and angry. He threatened to kill you and imprison me. I wanted you so badly, but you were away on campaign. I could only try and stay out of his sight. The rest is horrible dreams of darkness and feelings of dread and loneliness. I remember a dark place and there is something. No, there was someone there. I was not alone Maximus." Her breaths became short and quick.

"There was someone else there. Someone…I don't know who it was. I didn't know what they wanted. I was frightened and I cried out for you." She shuttered and buried her face into her hands.

"I am sorry, my love. It pains me so to see you like this. You don't have to be afraid any longer. It is all over. You are safe. We are together. Nothing will harm you. You will never be alone, again." He folded his arms around he,r calming her breathing.

Maximus paused. "I must tell you the truth of the evil that had darkened our lives for so long. You must know this so we can bury it in the past." He paused again, took a deep breath and continued.

"Alturust made true on his threat. While I was away, fighting his war, to earn the fortune and prestige we would need for our life together, he sent assassins to murder me. It was only after I had foiled his plot that I found out he had put you to death." Jebella drew herself tighter into his body. He felt her tremble with the fear of her memories.

"I fell into a madness and at once deserted my post. My soul was on fire. My intention was to go to Emesa and avenge you by killing Alturust with my bare hands. I wanted to hold his treacherous heart in my hands and crush the life from it. All I could think of was vengeance."

"Word of my desertion and intentions got to Alturust before I got to him. He sent another force to ambush me. I survived the attack but, I was badly wounded. Injured and unable to complete my revenge. I lay dying, resigned to join you in the next life. A powerful Magus named Huron found me unconscious and near death. He saved me. As I began to regain my strength and sanity all I could think of was Altrust's death. Huron told me there was still life I was meant to live."

"But, I had to let go of my obsession for blood. He said if I traded life for death there was a way I could have you back. He took me as his apprentice, but treated me as a son. I was taught all he knew. This started my quest to learn the magic that would bring us back together. When he died, he passed along to me all that he was. I have used that knowledge and power to bring you back."

"How long was I gone?" she asked anxiously, not sure if she wanted the truth. "Tell me Maximus. How long?" Her grip on him increased with the fear in her voice.

"Ten years," he mumbled.

"Ten years," her eyes tuned into waterfalls. "Are you saying that I have been…?" She could not say the word. "That I was," she swallowed, "for ten years?" Jebella shook her head from side to side with disbelief. She looked at her arms and legs and ran her hand across her face.

"This cannot be possible. No, it cannot be true. Please," she begged. "Tell me this is a cruel joke or a fitful dream." She looked around franticly searching for an escape.

Maximus held her trembling form and wiped at the flow of tears.

"I am sorry, my love. It is all true. You are restored and we are reunited. Nothing can separate us again. My magic is strong, and my sword is sharp. I will defend our love against all foes." He drew back from her and looked into her eyes.

"Jebella, we are one. You are the other part of me. I have not been alive these longs years you were not with me. I died with you that day. I became a shell, a shadow, until today. There was no life in me until I saw that life breathed back into you. Now we live. Our life begins anew."

"Why have you done this!" she screamed. "I am a monster!"

"No, no Jebella. You are just as lovely and beautiful as you were the day I left you. Look see for yourself." Maximus handed her a seeing stone.

Jebella stared at her image, smoothing her hand across her face. Sweeping the tear-soaked hairs from her face, Maximus kissed her quivering lips. He pressed his body close to her. They melted into a tangle of limbs and caresses as they loved each other, late into the day.

Maximus awoke feeling as he had not in years. He reached for Jebella. She was not there. He sat up abruptly. Had he dreamt it all as he had so many times before? He desperately looked around. Jebella was sitting before the fire with her arms wrapped around legs pressed tight to her chest. She rocked as she stared blankly into the fire.

His heart relaxed and he laid back in relief. It was real. She had returned and all was well. Maximus watched her, absorbing her with his eyes, breathing her in as if she were air. This woman, this beautiful creature was all that mattered in the whole universe and he would rededicate the rest of his existence to her happiness.

As he watched her the look on her face began to worry him. "Jebella, what troubles you so? Tell me and I will make it better."

Without removing her eyes from the fire, she said in a slow chilling voice that sounded as if it came from far away. "You must send me back."

"Send you back?" He sprang to his feet. "There are no forces in the twelve realms that can make me do such a thing. No power will take you from me again. I would do battle with the gods themselves before I would do that." He softened his voice.

"You are still confused. Your mind is unsettled. Things will become clearer soon. Come, eat, drink and rest," he said, making way for her to return.

"I must go back, Maximus. I cannot stay with you. I have not felt whole ever since my return. A part of me is missing. I now know why. It is because of him. He is there alone. I must go back and be with him."

"With him? I am him. It is I, Maximus. You are mixed up. We

are together. There is no other. Please, let this go from your mind.”

“No,” she said firmly still staring into the fire. “You do not understand. He is there in that dark place and he is alone. All alone and frightened. I remember it all.” The tears were in her voice while her eyes remained clear and fixed on the flames.

“I remember my death. I remember the twisted smile on Altrust’s face as he plunged the dagger into my heart when I told him I loved you and he would never have me. He laughed as I called for you with my dying breath. His last words were a curse that we should be separated forever and never know peace.”

Maximus stood transfixed clenching his fist until his knuckles threatened to crumble from the pressure.

“I remember,” she continued, “being in an endless blackness. A cold, frightful place. I was not alone. There was something else there. For so long I did not know what it was, and I feared it. I kept calling for you. I began to realize it was not something, but someone. Then I began to understand.”

For the first time, she looked away from her other world and met his eyes. “I knew. I felt it. I held out my hand.” She extended her hand. “And he placed his in mine and it was right. It was our child, Maximus. Our son.” A tear ran down her cheek.

“When I died. I was with child. Our son died with me and we crossed over together. Because we were joined, he became trapped with me. There was only he and I and an endless blackness. Now he is wandering there alone.”

“A child? A son? Our son?” Maximus felt his legs go weak.

“Yes, our son.” Her eyes were filled with pain. “He is in that awful place. That nowhere. I must go back. He is alone and frightened.”

“My son. But…but I never knew,” was all he could say. The warnings from Huron fell upon him like a mountain of stones. The old magus warned him what he sought had unforeseen cost.

“All magic has a price, Maximus,” he cautioned. “The greater the desire, the greater the price. What you ask for requires enormous sacrifice. Think and think well before you go down that path. What you ask for may cost more than you are willing to pay."

Maximus was given that warning over and over again as he reached for greater and more powerful magic. Yet he continued his quest unafraid of the consequences; heedless of the dangers. A man possessed and single-minded, sees nothing, but his loss, his defeat; never the price of his victory. Only now did he understand the full cost of his actions. His mind raced about desperately hunting for answers, but all he found were walls with no door. Questions with no answers.

Was he to lose her and even more? This time by his own hands? Could he have recovered his treasure only to see it stripped away? Was it possible that the last ten years had been a cruel lesson? Had he asked for too much? Was his failure to taunt him forever? Was his hubris going to shatter his world? Maximus fell to his knees.

"No, I will not let this be. I will not give you up again. I will crack the world in two before I let this be." Maximus screamed a soul chilling howl. His heart stop beating.

Jebella ran to him and knelt beside him. "Maximus, you must. We cannot leave him there alone. He is our child. He is the other part of me, of you, of us. We are not whole without him. He cannot be left to wander alone and frightened."

"I cannot do this. Don't ask me such a thing. I will not," he shouted into his hands. "The gods cannot be so cruel. Ask me to rip the heart from my chest or tear my eyes from my head, but, not this. Please," he begged. "I cannot. I will not...I..."

"Unless you can bring to this world what was not born into it, you must. Can you do this? Can you create life? Can you give our child the life that was denied him? Can you refill this empty space?" She placed her hands over her empty womb. "Can your magic make a lost promise live?" The pain in her eyes told him she knew the answer.

"No," he whimpered. "If I had known. If I had more time. Maybe..."

"I can see you have become very powerful but, even your

powers have limits. You bought me back, but not him. He is no longer here." She said hugging her middle. "I am not all here."

Jebella spoke calmly, tenderly and with determined sturdiness. She gently cupped his face. "My love, there is no greater wish I have than to be with you. The thought of being without you pains my soul. Eternity with you is all I've ever wanted; all I've ever needed. Our love defies death, it knows no ends, no bounds. You have proven that. Our son is also proof of that. He is the result of our love. I cannot deny that love to our child. Without him we are diminished. I must go back. I must go to him. I don't want to be there. I don't want him to be there, but if he must be there then I must be there with him. I will not let him be alone. Please, I beg of you Maximus, don't ask me to forsake him." Her voice became as hard as a rock. "I cannot. I will not."

Maximus stood. The weight of her words held him like steel chains. Maximus turned away unable to meet her gaze. "I must think." He walked away. Jebella did not try to stop him. She stood and watched him walk away.

Hours later he returned and sat beside her. Placing his arms around her, he pulled her close to him. They stared into the fire together seeing different worlds; worlds where they were not together.

"I know what must be done." He said calmly, never looking at her. "A few more hours together and I will let you go." His voice was slow and measured, full of emotions.

"When you return," he hesitated. The words had been hard to say. "You and he will be free of that place. You will move on to the next world." Turning to face her he continued.

"I promise by all the stars that burn in the night sky we shall be together, you, I and our son in the next world." From a strength he did not know he had. Maximus gave a weak smile and asked. "What shall we name him?"

Her eyes lit up and she gave him a sad smile and nestled her head against his chest. They spoke no more words that night. The hours passed away with heart-sick kisses.

By noon the next day Jebella was gone.

Maximus sat staring at the empty altar. Her last words, "Goodbye, my love." And his reply of, "never," still echoed in his head. Maximus waited until the moon was high in the sky. He whispered to Jebella through the stars. "It will never end my love."

Maximus checked his dress, sheathed his sword, excited his magic, and headed to Emesa. His heart began to beat again.

THE SINGER

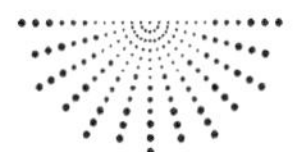

The marquee flashed "Slate Kingston-One Night-One Performance." A ticket awaited me at the box office. I settled in a corner table with a clear view of the stage.

The club was an intimate homage to the speak easies of the thirties. A room full of small tables and art deco gingerbread. The smell of flowery perfumes, stale beer, and weathered leather scented the air. The lights blinked out, plunging the club into total darkness. A spotlight emanated from the back of the stage silhouetting a black-clad figure. His iridescent eyes glimmered like distant galaxies. He scanned the room with a Cheshire cat smile.

"Good evening," rising from a three-legged stool, he sang. "I have loved you longer than the stars have burned. Felt you soul meld with mine. No space, no time between us. We are all the universe hopes to be."

His voice was like that of an old lover; soothing, familiar and comforting. He strutted across the stage weaving a dance of enchantment. A chill raced down my spine as I fell into the web he wove.

The room hushed to the silence of a tomb. His acapella crooning reached new heights as it floated through the air like a

Luna moth. It wings slowly, rhythmically stroking the air, stopping only long enough to lay a delicate kiss on your ear before fluttering away. The expression in his hypnotic elocution cast a spell of glamour over the audience. He did not ask. Nor did he need too. He was welcomed in. We threw open the doors and begged him to enter; surrendering body and soul.

His eyes twinkling like droplets of dew in the moonlight seemed only for me. The passion in his lover's gaze infected every woman and man in the room. He freely spread his charm among us. The shy blush of first-time nakedness with a new lover colored our cheeks.

"Transcending the limits of thought. Beyond the meaning of life and death. Deep in the abyss of desire. We live and die and live again," he sang. When he stretched out his hand, we all leaned forward to be the one to receive his touch. Our inhibitions melted away as surely as the ice in our sweating glasses. We were lost in a maelstrom of lust and adulation. We loved him. I loved it.

His song, his voice, was a primeval cry awakening long-forgotten memories of passionate liaisons. He moved something deep inside us. Stoking forbidden appetites into infernos of desire. The thrill raced through my limbs like liquid fire. Feelings of ecstasy and longing mingled in a sensual dance spurred on by this vocal foreplay.

My fingers, like all those in the room, found heat and satisfaction as we slowly traced along the naked flesh of our face, our neck, our arms and legs. Our skin grew moist and sticky. Women heaved expectant breasts. Hardened nipples brushed briskly against silk blouses. Skirts inched up higher exposing expectant thighs. Soft purrings rippled from dry throats. Hungry ruby red lips parted slightly gasping for air. Hair from evening up-dos cascaded down slightly undulating bodies.

Men jostled uncomfortably in their chairs, clenching their sweaty palms and noticeably panting. Nervously readjusting relaxing spines, they fought the impulse to peer into that forbidden room. Tapping nervous feet and wavering legs, they straightened their backs in an effort to maintain acceptable thoughts. Their guilty eyes twitched and blinked anxiously fighting the desire of carnal images.

Slate smiled and the temperature rose. He paused. The room held its breath. He closed his eyes, leaned back his head and whispered the sweetest moan. The room exhaled and sighed. Again, and again we were led to the edge, to the promise. Again, and again he held back leaving us wanting more. Riding our wavering emotions like a boat rides the surf. It was infuriating. It was torturous. It was delicious.

Sometime during the night, a quartet of musicians joined him on stage. We did not notice and would not have acknowledged them had he not asked for applause for them at the end of the set. The lighting again went black and he was gone. The anxiety in the room became palpable. What had happened? We were abandoned, jilted; as if he had left us standing at the altar. I wanted to rush the stage and find him, t ask him, "What did I do?" To beg him to "take me back."

As the enchantment began to fade, I could see my flush of cmbarrassment and abandonment reflected on the faces of all around me. I felt exposed as if my secrets had been laid out for public inspection. Contrite as if I had awakened in public naked. I imagined the entire room had shared my most intimate secrets. Like a teenager suffering the humiliation from the public reading of a love letter.

Straightening my disheveled clothes, I rushed out into the night air. The cool freedom hit me like a splash of cold water. Clutching my wrap around me, I could still feel his presence just as if his hand prints were tattooed onto my skin. Leaning against the rough brick of the building I took in deep breathes and began to regain my senses.

"Did you enjoy the performance?" came a voice from the shadows.

I looked into a playful pair of grey eyes that seem to look right through me. A curly haired youth with the fuzz of new manhood on his chin offered an impish smirk. I felt transparent. I stood erect, folding my arms like a blanket to hide my naked heart.

"Ah…yes," I stuttered, clearing my throat. "Your performance was delightful. I just needed some air. The room was getting a bit stifling." We both knew I lied.

"Shall we proceed with our business?" He pointed to a path leading away from the club. We walked a block to a gated apartment building and rode in silence to an upper floor. His apartment was much like him, youthful and unsophisticated. It was populated with large pieces of furniture and electronic gadgetry; displaying a taste yet unrefined.

"Will, the Directory…"

I interrupted. The professional rose to attention. "That is the last time you will ever mention that name." My tone was definite and stern. The surprise of his expression showed he wasn't used to hearing orders.

"From this moment forth your thoughts, your actions, your very being will be directed by us. You are being considered for inclusion in the most exclusive body in the world," I added. "This is an irrevocable membership. We will be all and everything to you." Our eyes locked in a battle of dominance.

"Slate Kingston will no longer exist. You will only be referred to from this point forward as The Singer."

He looked up at the ceiling. "The Singer, huh?"

I answered with a nod.

"I like it," he smiled. "Am I allowed the privilege of knowing your moniker?

"You may call me Stone."

"Just Stone?" he snorted in the tone of an arrogant rebellious teenager.

I leapt to my feet, the strength of granite on my face. His pupils enlarged with surprise as he felt the change come upon him. With just a slight adjustment of my focus, his limbs began to freeze in place. Slowly the effects of my powers seeped through his veins and made what was flesh feel like rock. His eyes full of disbelief and fright followed me as I paced before him.

For the first time, I felt I had the upper hand and it invigorated me.

"Singer, I am not like anything you have ever encountered. I could stop your heart with a thought. You would be found dead with no sign of the cause. There would be no hint of foul play. No need for investigation. Just another untimely death."

"This is not a game. There is no humor to be had. I am the last hurdle you must cross before you are officially accepted as one of us. You are young, undisciplined, and unpredictable. I have my doubts that you can handle the nuances of our work. But there are those who feel you have potential and could be a useful addition to our collective." I stopped and stared at him. "But I am not convinced."

"I have been given the discretion to decide what your fate shall be. To live and join us." I paused. "Or die and alleviate any possible future threat. The next few minutes will be vital to that decision."

The panic in his animated pupils told me he realized the gravity of his situation. I released my hold. He slumped back onto the sofa gasping for air, looking like a puppy disciplined for chewing shoes.

"I apologize. I have a tendency to use humor to mask my nervousness. I meant no disrespect," he panted, massaging his throat. I nodded. The victory for dominance was mine.

"That is quite a talent you have," he said.

"We all have our abilities. That is what makes our group so unique." Marching before him. I mentally dissected and reconstructed him. Considering his value and his liability, wary of what he lacked rather than pleased with what he had. He sat nervously, flexing here and there to make sure his parts still operated as before.

"There is one final hurdle. The most important of all. It will test your commitment and your strength of will." The Singer straightened and leaned in. "Let there be no ambiguity here. Your choice and your actions are a matter of utmost importance."

"You must eliminate something you love. Not just something trivial or mundane like a guitar or a photograph, but something of intrinsic value. Something that defines you. Something that will profoundly affect and alter you." I added, as he pondered the possibilities. "Or someone."

His head jerked up. He searched my face for understanding. "What? Someone? I don't understand. You want me to…?" His words faded as fast as did the blood from his face.

I resisted the desire to smile. "You sought us out. And went to great lengths to do it. You nearly exposed us and yourself to public scrutiny. Now we must find an adequate conclusion to your actions." Gathering my belongings, I moved to the door.

"We shall be waiting and watching. There is a time limit." I paused. "Decide quickly Decide correctly." I left the Singer sitting in a haze of confusion and shock.

The days turned into weeks and the weeks became three before we met again. "I had my doubts. I am pleased and a bit surprised that I was mistaken."

The Singer looked at me with placid eyes. His demeanor was flat and colorless. The aura of youth that had radiated from him was replaced by a subtle emanation of melancholy. His songs, even though still quite effective, were nevertheless disconsolate, somber, and more dark. He didn't exhibit the boyish playfulness that had disquieted me before. In a moment of weakness. Maybe a random twinge of misplaced maternal instinct or something else as irrelevant. I don't know. I felt the need to offer him a bit of solace.

Reaching for my neglected and under used muscles of compassion, in my most practiced voice, complete with a near authentic smile I said. "They were nothing. We are your family now."

SUPERSEDURE

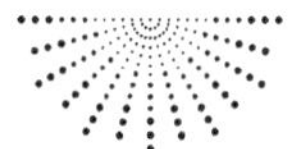

Carl was determined. The need within him thirsted without hesitation pulsing with the blind fury of desperation. The uncontrollable need animated desires kept under control by fragile bars of fear and guile. The hungers so primal and malicious the stench fouled the air, surrounding him like a swarm of ravenous leeches feeding on the juices of his decimated morals.

The mixture of delight and anticipation turned the sickness consuming his body into an elixir of youth; giving him power and purpose. The tissue around his joints swelled with pain and irritation. Bone scraped against bone. His head pounded with the force of a blacksmith's hammer. His skin was red with the flames of screaming nerves driven to exhaustion. Sweat seeped from his pores. The treason of disease working to contain him, would be denied.

Carl used the anguish. No obstacle would stand before his satisfaction. This one was the last. It would be the most satisfying. A surge of delight filled every inch of his five-foot frame quickening his steps. Pushing him beyond his pain.

Prowling the waterfront, his preferred hunting ground, he

found her. His prize awaited. She was the one. Young, fresh, and this was oh-so-important…alone. This was what had been calling him. This was the scream he heard in his dreams. Long flowing hair, smooth flawless skin, an air of innocence; she was perfect.

Peering from behind a camouflage of pine branches, saliva filled his mouth. He could taste the suppleness of her flesh, smell the tenderness of her youth, feel the warmth of her blood oozing from the corners of his mouth. Like a lion stalking a gazelle, a soft roar of ecstasy escaped his lips.

She leaned backward and shook her long blonde hair in the wind. There was a heaven in her movements. "I know you are there. I feel your eyes caressing me," she said without turning around. "I have come here night after night waiting for you to find me."

The edge of his surprise dulled. Carl felt a disappointment and a twinge of anger. He stepped from behind his blind. Their eyes meet. She did not shrink away. Her gaze beckoned him to her. His anger faded to curiosity.

Sweeping strands of hairs from her face, she walked toward him. His heart pounded. "I saw you, once. I stood where you are standing and watched you work. Since that time, I have needed to be with you."

Carl fondled the knife in his pocket. His fingers tingled as they slid across the cold steel. His breath deepened. A battle of anger, fear, and anticipation raged within him.

A familiar spark danced in her eyes. They were like mirrors reflecting his heart, his soul. Carl drew back. She smiled and kept approaching.

"I read everything wrote about you. I've studied everything said about you; every theory, every analysis." She stopped inches from him, licked her lips and whispered in his ear.

"One question. What is your name?"

Carl felt a connection he had never felt before. He wanted her more than any he had ever wanted before. He needed her. Without hesitation he surrendered to her call. Mouthing the word before he said it, "Carl."

She smiled. "Thank you, for the lesson…Carl. I'll take over now." She plunged a knife into Carl's heart.

A STEP TOO FAR

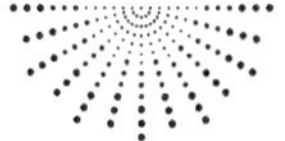

What's on the feed?"

"The coverage is broken and sporadic. They're giving conflicting details. All they're saying for sure is the mission was completed successfully. Nothing more since they yanked the visuals," replied Darryl. "I guess what they saw they don't like."

"They'll shut it down until they can come up with a scenario they want and can spin," Ken said.

"The television networks may be limiting coverage, but the radio waves are on fire," Zane said, jumping from station to station. "There's a lot of debate about what they actually saw." He looked at his companions with a face full of worry. "I don't like the way this is playing out."

"We knew there'd be strong reactions. It's all about the visuals, the symbolism, and what they represent. Images are powerful things. People have a visceral react to them. I'm sure some are scrambling to try and find a way to explain this away and others are cheering us on," said Ken. "There's no doubt we've shaken things up." He couldn't hide the uncertainty in his voice.

"Do you really think they know it was me?" Darryl asked.

"No doubt, big guy. What they're doing now proves it." Ken said.

"Isn't this what Elpis is all about?" asked Zane. "Hope. The last thing left in the box."

Ken smiled. "Yes, Pandora. That and more," he agreed jokingly.

"Hope, acceptance, expectation, a new way of looking at things, the possibilities can be…" His eyes darted about searching for a word. He settled on "transformative." "Some people are going to take this as a personal attack on them. Some will make it about their beliefs. The rest, the most, I hope, the ones I really care about, will see it the way we meant it and get something positive out of it."

"I agree. We wanted to make a statement and we did. They have no choice but to deal with it. It can't be taken back. Try as they might to hide it, the whole world saw it. It may be just a small thing, but it matters. We've made a difference." Darryl sighed. "It's up to the world now. Guys, I…" His voice trailed off.

"We know, man," offered Zane, nodding in empathy. "We all agreed. No matter what happens, we're in this together." The trio reached out and bumped clenched fists in a show of unity.

"Ken, you gave up something special," Darryl said with a touch of apology in his voice. "After all you were the chosen one."

"I'd rather be known for being a part of what we've done. This is so much more important. That's the history I want remembered." He swiveled his chair to face Darryl. "You better steel yourself, man. After all the scrutiny you'll have to face, you may not want to thank me. It's going to be intense and no doubt some of it will be ugly."

"I know. I am beginning to think of myself, a little, as a sacrificial lamb," he said, managing a weak smile.

"Well, fellas. You better take it all in. One more good look," Zane added, staring out the porthole. "I don't think we'll ever get the chance to come back up here again."

"If we've helped that beautiful blue ball from tearing itself apart, I'm satisfied. It's worth the price." Ken offered. Each man stared out the porthole, lost in their own private thoughts.

"Calvary Base. This is Elpis. Captain Kenneth Potts at the helm. Pre-entry check complete waiting for the okay to proceed."

"Calvary reading you loud and clear. All systems A-Okay. Commence with reentry."

"Reentry protocol in 5, 4, 3, 2, 1," counted Ken. "Firing aft thrusters."

"Altitude adjustment in progress, moving to course 324.5 by 58.137 alpha," added Zane.

"Pressure stable, beacon active, the board is solid," added Darryl.

"All system locked. It's a go. We're coming home. See you on the other side." Ken signed off.

The craft sliced through the stratosphere like a lightning bolt thrown by Zeus hurtling to deliver judgement. Splash down occurred at 12:59 pm UTC, July 24, 1969, in the Pareon Ocean. Helicopters arrived and hovered over the craft. Divers descended into the water and attached mooring lines, securing the vessel. The battle cruiser, URR Hornet, moved in to retrieve the capsule and its occupants.

Removing their helmets, the three shared a moment of solidarity before popping the hatch. Kenneth Potts emerged from the opening and was aided onto a raft headed for the cruiser. Zane Martin followed consigned to another raft. Darryl Bronson ascended through the hatch. A prick on the arm, a look of shock, and Bronson tumbled into the water and sank. Divers descended, attached rigging, and hauled him back to the surface. He was dumped onto a raft and transported to the cruiser.

News reports blanketed the air waves of the triumphant return of the space craft Elpis and its crew. The death of Darryl Bronson was reported as an aneurism caused by the unusually high g-forces during reentry.

"What were you thinking?" asked Paul Scott, Director of SEPSA (Space Exploration and Planetary Security Administration). "This stunt is going to cost you and Martin dearly."

"It has already cost Darryl dearly," Ken spit out.

Scott shuffled uncomfortably. "I don't like what you're implying." He paced in circles. "My God, Ken, you've opened a stinking can of worms that has fouled up everything. There are some very powerful, very unhappy people involved in this. This was supposed to be a pivotal moment in history. A moment for the record books."

"It was! It is!" Yelled Ken. "Just not the way you expected."

"You're supposed to be an astronaut not a damn social activist. You had the audacity to use what is the biggest event in human history to make a damn social statement…unbelievable."

"Don't you understand what it means for the world to see Darryl be the first? It would help level all playing field and elevate so many. The optics alone say so much. The social ramifications…"

"I don't want to hear that save the world bullshit!" snapped Scott. "You've really burned your ass on this. Your career is over. You're done." He passed his hands over each other like an umpire calling a base runner out. "You and your comrades have at best set the program back fifty years; at worst you've killed us all. You've caused a lot of good people a lot of grief. For some of us this was our life's work, and now you've gone and ruined it with this do-gooder nonsense."

"Nonsense? Do you…"

"Yes, nonsense. You'll be lucky if they don't hang you up by your self-righteous balls." He paused and rubbed his forehead, his eyes darted about as if their motion helped power his thoughts. "There's already a campaign under way to clean up…"

"Don't you mean cover up?" Ken interrupted. "How could you do this to him? You knew him. He was your friend. You worked with him…"

Scott jumped in and fixed him with a look of contempt. "I'd advise you to cooperate and forget all that. This is going to mean trouble for more than just you. Didn't you give any consideration to what this might do to your family and friends?"

Ken wanted to say that he did this for his family, his friends, and the whole damn world, but he realized that his words were falling on deaf ears. He hung his head and mourned his lost friend.

"They may need you at the moment, but your usefulness has a limited life span. Don't make things any worse than they already are."

Televisions and radios were flooded with experts, pundits, critics, politicians, religious figures, and apologists alike; anyone who could be trusted to tow the prepared line. The landing video was edited, certified, and reissued on the pretext of clearing up the images. Reinterpreted stories were created and attested to. Potts and Martin were coerced with threats of prison time and subtle hints of harm to their families. They were pressured into signing prepared statements and to upholding nondisclosure agreements. The new scenario was rehearsed until it became second nature to them, and they could recite it as if they believed it.

The evening of July 27, 1969 at the SEPSA news briefing, grief-stricken and haggard-looking Kenneth Potts and Zane Martin were paraded in front of the press, dressed in their honorific finest. Both men stood at attention with solemn faces and empty eyes. The event was televised all over the planet. Astronaut Captain Kenneth Potts was championed as the first man on the moon. The first human to step onto another world. Mammoth sized pictures of the blond haired, blue eyed hero arrayed in medals, ribbons and epaulets papered the walls. The ideal symbol of the indomitable spirit of man.

Astronaut Navigator Zane Martin was heralded as the second man to accomplish this historic feat. His pictures also adorned the walls, suitably attired. Darryl Bronson was given a cursory mention, devoid of pictures, enthusiasm, and sincerity. A flag hanging at half mass was his solo memorial.

After the news briefing, Potts was sent on a three-year assignment to a remote research outpost in the northern most region of Rimeland. Martin was assigned to a three-year tour of duty at a secluded nuclear test facility on the island of Mandarell in the Callivog Sea.

July 21, 1979 at 20:18 UTC; ten years to the minute; a somber solitary figure stood before the tombstone of Dr. Darryl Bernard Bronson. He held a hammer and chisel. Potts bent down on one knee. Teary eyed he chiseled under the date of death, "First Man on the Moon."

1 7

PEACE OF STONE

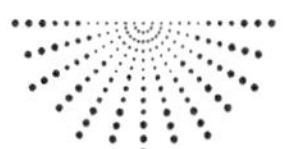

"What's my name, freak? Say it. Mr. Collins. King Collins. Say it!"

"Bobby's fist," was what I thought. Instead of saying it, I just hung on the end of his left arm staring at his right fist. I had become very familiar with that fist. It was introduced to me three years ago and has come to visit almost daily. At first, I fought back, but the more I did the longer and harder the beatings became. If I complained to anyone, Bobby found new ways of "giving me what I deserved" as he called it. After a while I learned to just take it.

When he drew his fist back from my nose it was stained with droplets of blood. I stared at the red stains, surprised I could still bleed.

"You like that freak?" he punched me in the eye.

"Come on, Bobby," one of his buddies called. "We gotta go." Bobby Collins' fist turned into a pointing finger. "You better be happy I've got more important things to do, dweeb." He laughed. "I'll see you tomorrow. I promise." Bobby threw me to the ground. I laid there until he and his laughing friends walked away.

Gathering my scattered books and papers, I didn't make a sound. I've learned to stay quiet. My whole world has become quiet. I know when people notice you, when people notice you, they hurt you. So be quiet. Be like stone. Like a statue, still and quiet. When I'm a statue, I'm safe. Stone never hurts.

I slowed down when I saw Calvin's car—he was my moms' current boyfriend--in the driveway. The house smelled like smoke and musty socks. A couple of empty vodka bottles and a six-pack with only one beer left lay beside the couch. An empty pizza box full of cigarette butts and ashes sat on the table. Mom and Calvin were twisted together on the sofa like pretzels. He was wearing boxers and one white sock. She was in her panties and a bra. Her hair looked like a ragged dust mop. Their eyes were red, and half shut. They were cursing and laughing over the noise of the television.

"Hey little man. Did you run into a little trouble on the way home? Calvin joked, pointing at my black eye.

I stood silent with blood on my shirt, dirt on my face, and hate in my eyes.

"Didn't you hear him ask you a question?" my mother sputtered, as she stumbled to her feet. She came over and poked me in the shoulder with her fingers.

"Fighting again, I see. You're as stupid and useless as that no-good father of yours. Someday you'll end up in prison just like him. If you didn't look so much like him, I'd wonder if they didn't give me the wrong baby at the hospital. Knowing what you'd turn out to be I should have left you there."

"Aw, leave the kid alone," Calvin threw his car keys at her. "Here." The keys struck her in the back and fell to the floor.

"Go to Mark's and get us another bag. Ain't but one joint left." She picked the keys up from the floor, almost falling over. Righting herself, she grabbed her dress, threw it over her head and zigzagged toward the door.

"Stop and get another bottle, too," Calvin yelled before she slammed the door.

I ran into the bathroom to wash my face. When I looked up into the mirror Calvin was standing behind me. I froze. *"Why didn't I lock the door?"* He locked it for me and began dropping his shorts. I tried to move around him, but he grabbed my shoulder. His fingers dug into me as he held me in place. "Where you going Josh? I thought you and me was friends?"

"I don't…"

He squeezed my shoulders even harder and said, "Sure you do. Like I said this is what friends do for each other. I would never steer you wrong, buddy. I promise." After he left, I laid on the floor. The cool tiles against my face drawing the pain away until I was cold as stone and didn't feel anything.

I laid there thinking about running away, again. There was nowhere or no one to run to. If I made trouble it would only mean more problems for me. I wanted to cry and yell, but it wouldn't change anything. Besides statues don't cry. Statues don't hurt. Statues are quiet. Statues don't care. *"Be a statue."*

I got up from the floor, slipped out the backdoor, and ran to the park. I wanted get to my special place, the hollow rock under the bridge. It was my secret place away from the world. I'd go there to be safe and be alone.

In the shadow of the bridge no one could see me. There are nights I slept there when my mom and Calvin were fighting. Especially the times when my mom was away, and Calvin and I were home alone.

From my hiding place, I can see the statue by the flag pole. It's represents some soldier nobody remembers. He stands there silent and uncaring, no matter the weather, no matter what happens. I try to be him."

"What's wrong?"

"Nothing," I said without thinking.

"I can see that something is making you sad. Why don't you tell me about it? Maybe I can help?"

I looked up and nobody was there. "Who said that? Where are you?

"Here. Here I am." I heard water splashing.

I looked down to the water's edge. There was at a boy about my age peering out of the water. He had long black hair and two deep dimples that sat under sky blue eyes. His chest was bare, and his skin was pale as milk.

"You'll catch your death," I said. "Even in Georgia it's too late in the year to be skinny-dipping. Look at you. You've already pale as a ghost."

He laughed and said, "This is my regular color, and this is where I live."

"Under the bridge?"

"No, silly. In the water. Not here, though, in the ocean. I just got here." He swished his tail out of the water and dove under. I jumped up and ran to the water. He reappeared. "You're a mermaid!" I exclaimed.

"I'm a merman," he corrected me. "My name is Alotus. What's yours?" His smile returned.

"I'm Josh."

"Glad to meet you, Josh. Tell me why you are so sad?"

It's nothing," I said staring at my feet. "I just need to be older." I looked at him. "In a few years I'll move away, and things will be better."

"Everyone should be happy." he said, as if it was obvious. He talked with a voice that sounded like singing. It put me at ease. "Why don't you just leave now?

"I'm only eleven. That's too young to get a job and take care of myself."

He thought for a moment. "Is there nothing else you can do?"

I shook my head no.

His face lit up as if he had just discovered the most wonderful thing ever. "If you're so unhappy why don't you come live in the ocean? You can be happy there. There's plenty of room. You won't need a job or anything."

"That sounds really nice but, I can't. I can't live under the water like you."

"Don't worry about that. We can fix that. We'll make you so you'll be like me. We know how. You and I can be best friends. We'll play with the dolphins and ride whales. It'll be fun. I promise."

"I don't know." I stuttered.

"Don't be afraid. It won't hurt. It'll be great."

"What would I have to do?"

He held out a hand to me. "Just come on down into the water with me."

I inched to the edge of the water and looked down at him. The upper half of his body was smooth like a catfish. The bottom half was covered with blue and green scales that ended in a big tail. The scales shimmered as the water passed over them. He smelled old and salty like the ocean.

I looked at his hand for a long time before I reached out and took it. It was cold and slick like holding an ice cube. I pulled back a little. He just smiled and inched me forward. The water began to fill my shoes. I kicked them off and felt its coolness crawl up my legs. I stiffened from the chill.

"Come on Josh. We're going to have so much fun," he said, as he guided me further from the shore until the water was up to my chest.

I started to panic and pulled back.

"Don't stop now. Come on," he urged me. "It may get a little scary. Just close your eyes and hang on to me. Everything will be alright. I promise."

His smile helped my panic to ease. I looked deep into his eyes. They were the hard eyes of a statue. I was no longer afraid. I would be a statue, too. I wanted it this. I'd be free. No more disappointments. No more promises. No more pain. I closed my eyes, held my breath, and let him guide me deep into the lake. We descended out to the middle of the lake, settling on the bottom. I opened my eyes. My lungs were aching for fresh air. I watched the bubbles of air begin to escape from my nose and my lips. I needed to breathe. The air erupted from me. I drew in the cool waters. My body jerked trying to spit it out. I fought the urge and sucked it in deeper.

Alotus was floating in front of me. His happy expression turned into a laughing sneer. He began swimming around in circles pointing and laughing. I grinned as the life began fading from me. Alotus stopped in front of me. He couldn't understand why I wasn't fighting. Why I wasn't flaying in the water like a fish on dry land. Why I wasn't trying to reach the surface. He watched me calmly let go. I stiffened and hung suspended as if I was a portrait on the wall. An expression of peace frozen on my face. I went stiff. Like a statue.

My new friend swam away leaving the statue to lay on the bottom.

18

ANOTHER ONE, SAM

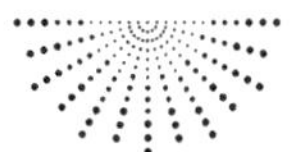

Henry took a stool at the bar. "What you having?" asked Sam.

"A Bloody Mary," he groaned, baring his teeth.

A few moments later Sam returned with his order. "Is a Bloody Helen okay?"

Henry nodded and bit in.

THE TREATMENT

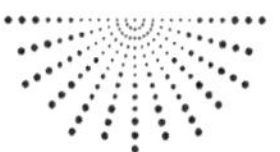

Our home has been trampled and broken. Clotting blood is the only remaining remnant of life. Like shards of broken glass, the twisted bodies of my fellow settlers lay around me. I know that I am the last of us. The last of my kind. We have become a dead race, a lost taxon.

My wounds are deep and fatal. I am consumed by a numbness that leaves me hollow. As the last bit of life seeps from me, I can no longer mourn. It is beyond me. Regret and sorrow serve no purpose now that the deed is done.

Desperation consumed us as we battled for our lives. Trying to find a reason for this chaos. As we wrestled with the whys, our attackers answered with the hows. How to remove us. How to kill us. How to wipe us from the world. We were two forces racing toward a wall with no doors. Both trying to reach a goal that would lead to the destruction of the other.

Our world is on fire. This oppressive heat began just before the first attack. It raged on, growing ever hotter. Everything went white as if our souls were set to flame. It's like the heat of a fever that comes with delusions and fits. Even the ferocity of our anger could not match this inferno. This pyrexia is a nightmare dreamt while awake, a vision of ruin and destruction. The atmosphere steams, gurgles and flows with it. It's a fog made of burnt wishes and smoldering hopes. My thoughts whip between fury and sorrow, agony and revenge, denial and disbelief. My indignation is both fluid and unending. And still the fever grows; ever higher; ever stifling.

First came the White Corps; only one or two at first. They routed everyone they encountered. Encircling their prey and ripping them apart like jackals. We pressed them back. Their numbers grew with their next incursion until wave after wave fell upon us like the surf against the shore.

We were not prepared. Coexistence, not war, is our way. There was no reason to deny our small patch of life. Our presence posed no threat. We did no harm. We are benign and only seek to live. They would give no quarter. We battled, fell back, regrouped, countered, and fell back again. Back and forth we parlayed. Showing unending resolve, we hoped would give our attacker pause and change their aggression toward us. We soon realized that there was no middle ground. No peace would be found. No truce was possible. Fear and trepidation drove us as we saw this was not merely a battle. The ferocity of the onslaught showed us it was fight or die. Our enemies made it clear that total extermination was the only acceptable conclusion.

Hordes of Tees joined the onslaught. They came in clusters, attacking unmercifully. Slicing and tearing like sickles through wheat. They penetrated our walls, slashing all they encountered, spilling blood like raindrops in a storm. Our screams and shouts were for nothing, only death heeded our cries. Even after death they desecrated our remains, grinding our bodies to silt. Still the temperature rose. This fever fed them. We wavered and weakened in this life sapping swell. They reveled and grew bolder, basking in its flow, and gaining more power and more cruelty.

Our colony was a small one. We had not long settled in and were reaping our first harvest. We were pilgrims in a new world eager to establish ourselves. Our homestead was on fertile ground and our harvest was a meager one. In time we hoped to prosper and gain in numbers, to divide and multiply. They swept in like an ill wind and blew our hopes away. No one was immune, all fell to this preemptor. Despite our efforts no one was spared.

We were vastly outnumbered but, we are a hearty race and do not fall easily. Our way is not one of ease. We are made to survive. We believe in the struggle. We absorb the challenges and adapt to the harshness of our trials. The difficulties of life are not new to us; we persevere. We fight for life because there is nothing else. Life is everything. We made it clear that even if we fell the cost of vanquishing us would be high. They ignored our machinations and persisted; oblivious to their own sacrifices. Relinquishing a number of theirs lives for one of ours. They never slowed, never doubted and never yielded. Their single-minded determination pushed forward. We recoiled at their mantra: "Kill, kill, kill them all."

After hard-fought days of battle, we dared to hope that our resistance had prevailed and there was a chance of survival. We would not be conquered. We hoped life would win out. To our horror they came with new weapons; new abominations.

At first, we thought we were weakening from prolonged battle. But no, it was their new weapons that caused our sickness. They released a hell spawn that oozed about us and burned like liquid fire. It took our breath, clouded our vision, choked, and seared us. We began to atrophy and die. Some roasted in their skins. Some blackened and curled. Some swelled and burst. Others spit forth their innards and bled out.

Old and young alike shriveled up and withered away. We were ripped away like weeds in garden. The strongest of us were able to resist, for a while. This liquid death crashed over us like a toxic wave. Scarred, crippled and depleted, we soldiered on. There was no denying it was only a matter of time.

In their zeal for victory, more unthinkable methods of destruction were unleashed upon us. Streams of light like fire were unleashed on us. Flame-like tentacles fell on anything they touched. They sapped the very essence from everything they touched. Hot and intense, as if the eye of the sun was staring us down. Burst of this killer gaze swept through our ranks and decimated what was left of us.

Not only did my brethren fall, but many of the enemy fell victim to the fatal ravishes of these death rays. The loss of their own did not halt their onslaught as long as we died. The destruction was so complete that you could not tell where one body ended and the other began. We laid blended together like some putrid batter. Many tried to shield themselves with the bodies of the dead but, the beams burned through and laid waste to the dead and the living. Some sizzled like grease on the fire. Others pruned and flaked away and some just fade from existence.

With no weapons to match this awesome force, our efforts were in vain. No crack or crevice provided protection. We were sought out in all places and eradicated. No matter how noble the effort, our end was written. Our home was overcome, plucked out like a rotten fruit from a barrel. We were undone. The purge was complete.

Wasted and over whelmed, I saw the end in sight. I tried to summon up a miracle. I tried to believe into reality that survival, at least was possible. I could do no more than watch our tomorrows fall to fat; to melt away like melting snow.

The end was not swift. Death lingered like the smell of smoke. A last sigh and I surrendered to inevitability. A bloody mixture of sweat and tears, I let death wash me away.

"Mr. Hamilton," the doctor said with a triumphant glee. "I am pleased to say the cancer is in total remission."

20

EUSTIS

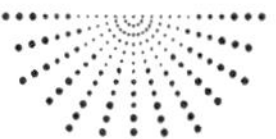

I am Eustis. I honestly don't know what I am. I have been any countless number of things. Once I was a young girl tending goats on a Bolivian hillside, once a swallowtail butterfly in a field of Kansas sunflowers. I was a renaissance painting hanging in the Louvre, a young yak calf in Mongolia, another time I was an old man with dementia in a Florida nursing home. I've been a pregnant woman swollen with twins, and a plastic water bottle in a recycling bin. I was once a single-celled bacteria living on the walls of the Marina Trench, a child soldier at war in the Congo, and even an asteroid hurtling through the Kuiper belt.

Without any thought, effort, or intent, I am obliterated and become something new. It seems I'm everything and nothing. I exist for a day, a week, a month or longer, and then I die, or am destroyed, or simply fade away. As I did when I was a cumulus cloud over the Sahara dessert. I always…always end. And in a flash my new reality begins.

When I was a child soldier I was gunned down in battle. As a bulldog, I was run over by a bus. As a '57 Chevy, I was stolen, stripped for parts, and crushed for scrap. A pack of hyena tore me to shreds on the savannah when I was a zebra.

I was a nebulous cloud of gas floating in interstellar space shaping planets and stars. When I try to explain who or what I am, I feel like I did when I was a deer trapped by on coming headlights; startled confused and paralyzed.

I am an infant who is aware of his world, but weak and helpless; powerless to effect it. Still I feel the power and potential of creation surging through me.

I don't know why this is happening to me and have even wondered if I might be insane and only imagine these lives. Imaginary or not, this is my existence.

It makes me wonder. Is this life? Is this how you're born? Jumping from one consciousness to another until you find the right fit for you? Or is this my own private version of hell? Am I being punished for some past transgressions? Did I commit some unspeakable sins that have damned me to endless cycles of life and death?. Or could I be cursed; the vengeance of a jilted lover or a defeated rival.

Maybe, I'm not crazy and this is the journey my existence is supposed to go through on its way to…whatever my life is to be? Is this actually a blessing, a gift? Is this immortality? Am I blessed to experience the depth and breadth of all there is? Or am I cursed to live an endless existence of chaos and change?"

There is no teacher or mentor. No voices or signs; only the example of experience.

Could I be a god-in-training learning all varieties of life before I am given dominion over them? Or maybe a fugitive hiding from a pursuer by jumping in and out of lives to hide my location? Or even a lost soul unmoored and doomed to drift on the wind of change?

I can't help but feel that with each life I am somehow changed; altered as if each incarnation, each span of time, is a lesson, or even a test. As if, maybe, I am being prepared for a greater challenge or a greater destiny, I cannot say.

I am Eustis. I am everything.

21

A NEW SPIN

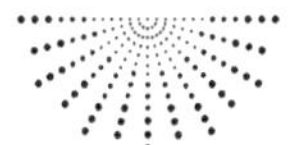

"Come on, Tellis. You can do this."

"I just can't do it, Layla. No matter how I try my webs always end up looking like confetti."

Layla pulled at the threads of silk. "It's really not …that bad. It can be fixed if you just angle this thread by about 35 degrees and add another one on a 10-degree axis to reshape this one. Then connect to this one…."

Tellis folded his legs and collapsed onto the ground. "It's no use. I just don't get it. I'm a failure as a web spinner. I'm a failure as a spider."

"Don't say that. You're an Orb Weaver; of course you can spin a web. It's what we've been doing for millions of years. It's in your DNA. It's just simple math. Simple geometry. You just have to concentrate and practice more."

"I have practiced, Layla. The math doesn't make sense to me. When I picture it in my mind, all the numbers and angles run together, and I end up with this."

"Just look, one more time." Layla began spinning silk. "First you make an anchor line, then you connect the next line to create a right angle. Then this one goes perpendicular to the anchor line and this line is parallel to the radius of the circumference of the diameter…"

Tellis compound eyes glassed over.

A Black Widow spider hanging from a nearby branch snickered. "How pathetic," she shook her head.

"Don't listen to her, Tellis. Spinning webs is overrated," Elmo said, walking onto the scene.

"That's alright for you, Elmo." Tellis replied. "Daddy Long Legs don't spin webs, but I'm an Orb Weaver. Spinning webs is what we're supposed to do."

"Who said you have to be like everybody else?" Elmo asked.

"It's the way it's always been, Elmo," Layla said. "Are we still spiders if we don't spin webs?"

"Don't listen to him. How would he know. His kind can barely be called an arachnid," the Black Widow shouted out.

"Go suck on a fly," Elmo shouted back. "Wolf Spiders, Crab Spiders, and Tarantulas don't make webs. So, you're saying they aren't real Spiders?" Elmo smirked, stretching to his full height, towering over the other two. "We all make silk. That doesn't mean we have to spin webs with it. There are other uses for it."

"But, I do, Elmo. It's my legacy. There's no way around it. I'm a failure as a spider."

"Look, Tellis you've got eight legs. You've got compound eyes. You can make silk. You're a spider. So what if you can't spin one of their kind of webs. Maybe you should spin your kind of web."

"What do you mean? My kind of web?" Tellis asked.

"I mean have you ever thought about doing it another way. Okay, the math confuses you. Forget the math. Do it the way you want to do it. There's more than one way to catch a fly."

"He may be right, Tellis," Layla piped in. "You've been trying to do it the way everybody else does it. Maybe you should forget them and do it your way."

"I've got a way?" Tellis asked

"Everybody has a way," Elmo said. "We're not all architects. We Daddy Long Legs just use silk to wrap our prey and our eggs.

Trap Door spiders spin trip wires. Tarantula use silk to line their walls and…"

"Real spiders spin webs," The Black Widow interrupted.

"Shouldn't you be out looking for a new husband?" Elmo shouted back.

"Don't listen to her," Layla said. "Elmo is right. Just because some of us make our webs a certain way doesn't mean you have to do it that way. How would you make a web if you hadn't been told how to?"

Tellis stretched out his eight legs and stood up. His compound eyes swirled around in their sockets as he thought for a moment. "I always thought making a web should be like more like growing a tree. Instead of worrying about angles, vectors and symmetry, it could…" Tellis drew a line of silk. With a swirl of his snippets, he arced another line and another and another until his silk lines started to look like the branches of a tree.

"That is different, Tellis, but it looks great." Layla screeched. "Keep going."

With her words of encouragement boosting his confidence, Tellis picked up speed and added more connections. One line grew out of another until there was a beautiful web shaped like a magnificent oak tree. Tellis stepped back and beamed with pride over his creation.

"That's what I'm talking about! It looks like a web to me," Elmo said.

"Tellis, it's wonderful," Layla added.

"Doesn't look like any web I've ever seen." The Widow said.

Elmo patted Tellis on the back. "That's because it's a Tellis original, granny."

UP ENDED

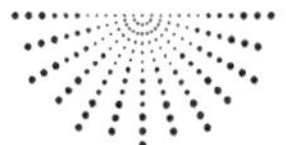

"Let's get a little closer, so we can get a better look at them."

"No way, man. I'm not getting any closer to those things. They look kinda…creepy. Besides, they could be dangerous. We could get bit or catch something."

"It's not like we're going to take one home."

"You're right. You're not putting one of those in my father's ship. I'd never get the smell out it. Let's go. I'll be in big trouble if I don't get this ship back before midnight."

"Yeah, yeah, just a minute. I wonder what they're called?"

"Ugly, if you ask me. Come on, man. I'm leaving with or without you.

"All right, dude. You're such a kill joy. Hey, you know what would be funny."

"What?"

"The probe. Ha Ha."

BOBOZAYLA

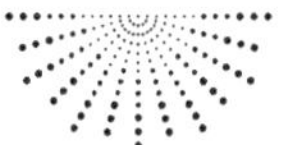

Howard and Terry jimmied their way through a back window. The old man was asleep in front of the television.

"Wake up, old fool." Howard yelled.

The old man roused and faced them. His dull brown eyes strained to focus on his intruders. He rose and stood motionless like a gnarled old tree. His expression was placid and bored as if he was hearing a joke he didn't find funny.

"Where's the money?" Howard growled pointing a finger in his face. "Don't make me hurt you, old man."

He reached his thin weathered hand into his pocket and pulled out three twenty dollars bills. Silently he held them out in cradled hands as if he was begging for more.

"Do you think this is a joke?" Howard slapped the money away. "I saw you withdraw five thousand dollars from the bank this morning and I want it. I want it now!" he demanded.

The old man shook his head. "The curse."

"The what!" Calvin shouted.

"The ibi…the evil," he answered.

"I don't give a damn about no ibi or no curse. I just want the damn money."

"I must bury the curse." The old man laid his hands across his chest. "The evil must die with me," he pleaded.

Enraged, Howard backhanded him across the face, sending him crashing into a corner table. The old man crumpled like a wad of discarded paper. He groaned and went limp. Howard stood over him heaving and panting.

"He…he's dead," stuttered Terry, staring from his perch against the wall. "You should…. shouldn't have hit him so hard. You…you killed him."

Howard spun with his fists raised. "Shut the fuck up!" He grabbed Terry by the collar, "don't you ever tell me what I shouldn't do. Who do you think you are? That drunken ass father of mine. Nobody tells me what to do. If you ever do it again it will be the last thing you ever do. Do you understand me?" He threw the smaller man to the floor with a punctuating, "bitch."

"Start looking around." Howard ordered. "Search everywhere. Find that damn money."

Cowering on his hands and knees, Terry scurried toward the bedroom like a bug escaping a raised foot.

Howard bent and began to search the old man. "You should've gave up the cash, old fool. It's all your fault. You made me do it. All you had to do was give me the money." He turned the lifeless body over and rifled through the pockets. A glint of light illuminated a burnished gold medallion protruding from under the ill buttoned shirt; a gold star with the raised image of an eye in the center and spikes surrounding it.

"What's this?" Howard ripped open the shirt. "Oww," he cried pulling his hand back as he pricked his fingers on one of the sharp points. Sucking on the cut he did not notice his droplet of blood absorb into the metal. Howard placed his knee on the withered chest and ripped the chain from around his neck. A shadow fell over the room. Howard felt a breath on his neck. He jerked around and looked over his shoulder. Nothing was there. Terry was in the bedroom. He was alone with the dead man. He brushed off the feeling and returned to work.

"This looks like real gold. I ought to get something for this.

Who knew the old fool was into bling?" He laughed, pocketed the medallion, picked up the three twenties, and went about ransacking the room.

Howard scrunched up his face. "It smells like the old fart in here, moth balls and liniment. You find the money?" He asked Terry as he entered the bedroom.

"All I found was must…musty clothes and du…dust."

"Go search the kitchen with your worthless ass. I'll take over here."

"It…it ain't here. I don't know what…he… he did with it. It ain't here."

Howard stared at him. In the dim light of the bedroom, his eyes glowed like smoldering coals. "Do what I say." His voice was flat and chilling. "Or do I have to teach you a new lesson?"

Terry tensed. With his back pressed to the wall, he slid from the room like a fly walking the ceiling. Howard upended the mattress, overturned the dresser, and tossed around items in the room as if he was a badger rooting for grubs. "What the fuck?" He read a fallen receipt.

"Pre-paid funeral services $4940.00. You bastard. You buried the fucking money. I'll just be damned."

"I should have jumped his old ass when I saw him this morning," he said, leaning against the doorframe of the kitchen. "If I didn't have that old bitch with me, I would have. She always in the way or needing something. I wish she'd just die."

"You don't…don't really mean that."

"You telling me what I think now?" He crossed the space between them and slapped Terry before he could beg for forgiveness. Terry swallowed his apology with the blow.

"Grab that bag of stuff. I got something more useful things for you to do with that stuttering mouth of yours other than saying stupid shit." he said, grabbing his crotch and exiting the back door. Terry rose from the floor and silently followed behind him. He winced when he caught sight of the fire building in the other room.

Howard spent a night of troubled dreams. His mind was full

of taunting laughter and murmured whispers. Drum beats pounded in the back of his mind. Smoke blanketed his vision. Sinister red eyes watched him from a faint ghostly face. Blood and bone and medal came together to form the medallion. It burst into existence born of flame and mist. The medallion dangled over him raining blood down covering him in a skin of red slime.

Howard struck out at the phantom whispering in the fog. The chants and drum beats increased like a racing heartbeat. He punched and kicked Terry, landing blow after blow causing him to take refuge on the floor. Howard fought until he snapped up into a sitting position drenched in sweat. With eyes full of confusion and fear, he gave up the battle and paced the floor the rest of the night.

As the dawn crawled over the horizon, Howard sat at the kitchen table seething like a pressure cooker. He was tired and didn't have the money. His muscles tense and jittery. Aimless angry thoughts raced through his mind. The medallion in his pocket warmed and pulsated as he became more agitated. The angrier he got, the warmer the medallion got until they were both a volcano ready to erupt.

The creaking steps of old bones entering the room grated on his already strained nerves. "Already with the drinking? Have you given up on food all together?" The voice gnawed on his sensitive nerves. "Look at you. Eyes all blood shot, hair sticking up all over your head, high on heavens knows what. Thank God your mother ain't alive to see what you've become." A percussion of clanking pots and pans joined the chorus as she continued to mutter and mumble her disapproval.

Howard squeezed the beer can harder and harder with every slight thrown his way. The medallion grew hotter. The whispers grew louder and clearer. *"She is against you. She is like the rest. They're all against you."*

"God knows I've tried, boy. I guess you just have too much of your father in you. I would be ashamed if I was you. 22 years old living in your grandmother's basement. No job. No future. What are you going to do when I'm gone? Live on the streets like a stray." She sneered at him like a cat looking at a mangy dog.

Howard flattened the can causing the beer to erupt over the table. He pounded the pointed edge into the table. Emboldened by the voice he shouted. "Shut the hell up, old woman. You're just like the rest of them. You're all against me. You never cared about me. You want to keep me down. You sour old bitch."

"Don't you talk to me like that, boy. This is my house. You..." Her squinting eyes shot wide open as Howard lunged and repeatedly planted the sharp metal into her chest. Blood splattered the wall and appliances. Her gown grew red with the blood from the jagged wounds he slashed across her body. She screamed and fell to the ground encircled by a growing pool of blood.

Somewhere between a whimper and a curse he cried. "You shouldn't have made me do that. A distant laughter echoed in his head. Encouraging him with faint praise. *She was just like the others. They are all against you. You were protecting yourself. Now you are free.*"

Howard laughed and cried cradling his head as he walked in circles around the body leaving a trail of meandering bloody prints. The medallion sent waves of energizing heat through his body. Its warmth was both comforting and frightening.

A horrified Terry silently backed down the stairs from his spying post at the top of the basement steps.

"Get up, Terry!" Howard shouted as he bound down the stairs. "We're outta here."

Terry stood frozen in the middle of the gloomy basement half in and half out of his hastily thrown on clothes. He eyed Calvin's blood soak clothes and trembled.

"What the hell is wrong with you?"

Afraid to speak, Terry just shook his head.

"We got things to do. Today things are going to change. Today things are going my way." He waved a bank ATM card in his face.

At the machine Howard withdrew the maximum. "Stupid old bitch. Don't you know you don't write the pin number on the card?" He laughed as he fanned the money around. "We'll go and ditch this stuff and it's party time. What do you say?" Terry nodded reluctantly.

"This is mostly junk. I'll give you fifty dollars for the lot of it." The pawn broker said.

"Fifty dollars, are you kidding me? This is some prime stuff, man. Antiques," Howard protested.

"Antique means more than just old. Antique means it's worth something. This is just random junk. Fifty, take it or leave it." Mr. Koppel said.

"What about this?" Howard produced the medallion.

Koppel felt the weight of it and turned it over examining it on all sides. "Where'd you get this?" His eyes widened with interest.

"You know, Koppel. Don't ask. Don't tell."

"Hey Jinja," yelled Koppel. "Come take a look at this and tell me what you think."

A short stout, no-nonsense woman wearing a dress that looked like a flowered tent sauntered from the back room. He held the medallion out for her inspection. She reached out to take it and quickly drew her hands back retreating several steps.

"Bobozyla. Bobozyla." Jinja made the sign of the cross and backed away. "Bobozyla," she whispered her eyes full of terror. "Get it away. That is the sign worn by the dammed. That thing is cursed. God protect us!" she cried.

The voice laughed in Howard's mind.

Koppel dropped the medallion to the counter and wiped his hands on his pants. "Take it back." He used a stick to push the medallion back across the counter. "Take all of it back. You would bring this evil into my store," he scowled. "Get out. Get out now."

"You crazy old bastard. It's just a fucking piece of jewelry."

"You don't even know what you have do you?" Jinja yelled. "It's cursed. Evil inhabits that amulet. It is worn by one who has made a pact with evil. Now you have it. You inherit the curse. Get it away from this place. Get out!"

"They are like the rest. They're against you. Kill them. Kill them before they kills you," Whispered the voice.

Howard started to reach over the counter, but Koppel was

faster. He reached under the counter grabbed a sawed off shot gun and shoved it in Howard's face. "Take your evil and get out or I'll blow your damn head off."

Howard snatched up the medallion and backed toward the door. "I'll get you for this, Koppel. You just wait and see you'll be sorry just like the rest. You think you can crap all over me. I'm not some punk you can treat any way you want," he roared, beating on his chest. His face contoured into something unrecognizable. Howard spit on the floor and stormed out the door.

"You too, little man. Go with your friend," Koppel said to Terry pointing the gun at him and shooing him away. "Take your things with you. May God have mercy on your souls," Terrys' eyes begged to stay, but he hung his head, grabbed the bag, and followed.

Terry met Howard in the alley behind the pawn shop. He was pacing from one building to another mumbling and swearing. "I'll kill that son of a bitch and his little black whore. You just wait and see. They can't treat me like some bitch. I'll…"

"Howard get rid of it p…please. Throw it in the riv…river. I…I think they're right. Some…something is wrong with that thing." Howard stopped pacing and stared at him like he didn't know who he was. "P…P…please Howard it's making you act stra…strange."

Howard stared at him. Then at the medallion. "You turning on me too? You're on their side? Is that how it is? Huh?" He shoved him against the wall of the building. His eyes becoming as red as fire.

"Nooo… It…it's just…"

Howard struck him with the medallion embedding the spikes into his neck. Blood squirted out like geyser. Terry screamed struggling to get away.

He is one of them. We do not need him. He is nothing.

Howard held him against the building stabbing him again and again shouting, "You're nothing. I don't need you. I don't need anyone."

"Hey what do you think you're doing? Stop it. You're killing him!" Howard turned to see a man running toward him.

"They are all coming to get you. Stop them." Like a wild animal fighting for its life, Howard leapt on the man and began stabbing him with the medallion. "You're all out to get me. But I won't let you. No. No."

A woman screamed and a crowd began to gather. Howard looked up and saw the descending mob. His eyes blind with madness, his clothes painted with blood and two mangled bodies lying at his feet., he growled at them like a mad dog and ran. The voice laughed and mumbled encouragement in his head.

"Call the police!" someone shouted.

"He went that way!" another shouted.

"There he is!" came another voice.

Screams, shouts, and the sounds of pursuit followed him. The whine of police sirens echoed off the walls of the densely packed buildings. Howard ran like a gazelle escaping a pride of lions. The noise of the mob grew louder. Howard ducked into the open door of an abandoned building. He searched desperately for somewhere to hide. Ascending metal stairs, he climbed to the roof. Police officers closed a net around the building.

"There's nowhere left to run, son." pointed out the police officer as he approached Howard on the roof, his gun drawn and hanging at his side. "Just give up and you can get out of this alive."

"I'm not your fucking son. Stay back!" Howard yelled, backing away. "You're not taking me. It wasn't my fault. They deserved it. They were out to get me." The medallion went cold. The fire left his eyes. Howard's head began to clear, and his eyes filled with tears. He looked around and pleaded. "It wasn't me. It made me do it."

"Okay. Just get down on the ground and put your hands behind your back. We'll go down to the station and straighten this all out."

"No. It wasn't my fault. I'm innocent I'm telling you!" he yelled. "See it was this." Howard began reaching for his pocket.

"Don't do it." The officer yelled. "Keep your hand away from your pockets." Howard started toward the officer his hand going for the medallion. "Stop!" screamed the officer. "Keep your hands up."

The medallion heated. The voice laughed. Howards' expression went from sorrow to rage.

"He's going for a weapon," another officer yelled. The officer planted a bullet in Howard's chest. Howard staggered back and teetered on the edge of the roof. Wavering in the wind like a limp flag, he fell six stories to the concrete alleyway below.

The voice laughed.

"This will be just a routine autopsy, Michael. I'll let you set things up. Just strip him down and catalog his possessions. I need to talk to someone in IT about our crashing computers. I'll be back in about 30 minutes. We can get started then."

"Sure doc. I'll have everything ready by the time you get back." The medical examiner left the room.

"Okay fellow," Michael said. "Let's see what you got. Keys, cigarettes, lighter, nail clip and... Whoa. Where did you get this? A nice wad of hidden cash, huh." He looked around. "Nobody will know if I donate this to the 'Michael is a poor college student fund.' You won't mind will you, buddy? Of course, you won't. After all you can't take it with you." He laughed depositing the booty into his pocket.

"Back to it then. Now what the hell is this? Man, you're full of surprises. This is an interesting piece of jewelry. I bet Janice would love this. Clean it up and birthday shopping is done." He flicked the air as if checking off a list. "Thank you." He looked at the identification tag. "Thank you, Howard. You have been a most helpful client." As he shoved the medallion into his other pocket, he pricked his finger on one of the spikes. A drop of blood vanished into the medallion.

The voice laughed and the medallion began to heat. Thirty minutes later the medical examiner returned to the morgue. Michael heard him enter the outer office. His eyes glowed. He picked up a scalpel.

The voice laughed.

NICE GUY

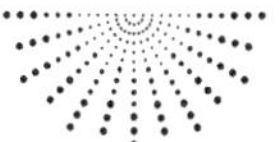

Harold was fresh out of Mill Creek High School in Pine Ridge, Missouri. I graduated from Our Mother of Immaculate Conception Catholic Academy for Girls in Boston, Massachusetts. We were both bound for our first taste of freedom and a collision at the University of Michigan. Curious, eager and naïve; we met, connected, and fell in love.

My prince charming was a lanky, incurably chipper, big eared, blue-eyed man-child. He was like a big clumsy puppy dog. Everyone who met him loved him.

I, his princess, was petite, unstylish, and woefully shy. We were inseparable. We studied together, ate together, and eventually slept together. Admittedly, awkwardly at first, but we figured it out to pleasing success.

Despite all the odds. I had snagged the last "nice guy" standing.

My parents fell in love with him, immediately and gave their unqualified approval. They both agreed he was such a "nice guy."

Harold's parents were equally enamored by me. I thought they would marry us right on the spot. From the moment we met I was their daughter and wedding plans commenced immediately.

After graduation we had a fairy tale wedding. Harold got a job with a pharmaceutical company and I went to work for an insurance agency. We purchased a two-story brick colonial in the suburbs. Three perfect kids came in quick secession; two boys, Mark and George, and a girl, Emily. We got a golden lab for the boys and a finicky white Persian for Emily. Life was perfect.

One Saturday in July, Harold was mowing the lawn and had a massive heart attack; a weak heart valve ruptured. Our fairy tale had become a Greek tragedy.

Everyone mourned his passing. The church was standing room only. The sanctuary was awash with flowers and letters of condolence. The testimonials were touching and many. People showered me and the children with so much sympathy it became unbearable. For weeks and months, we kept hearing how people missed him and how Harold had been such a "nice guy."

After wearing my widow's weaves for six months, I threw them out and returned to work. Harold had left a hefty insurance policy, but I needed something to do other than be the widow of the deceased "nice guy."

One Sunday after church I dropped the kids off to spend the day with their grandparents. I planned to enjoy a relaxing kid-free afternoon. When I got home, sitting on the patio in the suit he was buried in, was Harold. I know how this must sound. He had died. But, almost one year to the day after he kicked the preverbal bucket; Harold was back.

After an hour or so of screaming, crying, and hyperventilating, I asked the obvious question "Harold, what are you doing here?"

He looked at me puzzled. "I live here."

Weaving through the maze that was the headache consuming my brain I said. "But, Harold you're not living at all. You're dead."

Harold looked at me with those pleading puppy eyes and said in his most sincere deadpan style, "But, I feel fine."

I have always tried to be levelheaded. I am not prone to hysterics, but if your dead husband shows up out of the blue, I think you have the right to freak out, at least a little. Dumbfounded, I could only stare at him in a state of total disbelief and amazement.

This had to be a cruel sick joke. Some jealous vindictive person had hired a look-a-like actor to dress up and play Harold to torture me. I called the police. They came and pulled their guns at the sight of him. The Harold look-a-like was taken to the police station. He was fingerprinted, interrogated, and brought back. The officers said he checked out and yes it was really Harold. "Sorry ma'am. There's nothing we can do. There's no law against being dead." They mentioned how cooperative he had been and what a "nice guy" he was even if he was dead.

"Well thank you so much officers, you have been no help at all."

I was beyond unnerved by now. I didn't know what to do. I called our priest. If this situation had not been so dire it would have been one of the best moments I've ever experienced. The look of total horror on the priest's face when he saw Harold was priceless. Let's just say I'm glad I don't have to do his laundry. He threw holy water on him. Nothing happened; just a wet Harold. He tried to exorcise him. When that didn't produce any results, he reluctantly sat down with him. They talked and prayed and even shared a laugh. He shrugged his shoulders. "He's Harold alright. He's not a demon. He's not possessed. He's just the same "nice guy" he always was. He's just dead." With that, he made the sign of the cross and ran off like he had been caught stealing from the collection plate.

"Well thank you, Father. I am so glad you could visit. Maybe the next time you come by you might actually do something useful."

Here was the man I vowed to love 'til death us do part, and he wasn't parting. I had lived up to my end of the contract. Was there some technicality that I had missed in the small print on the marriage license? Or maybe I was being punished for some transgression in my past, some karmic faux pas I wasn't unaware of?

It's not that I didn't love Harold. I did and I do; it's just the dead thing. It doesn't work for me. Am I a bad person because I don't want to be married to a dead man? Is it too much to want your husband to be alive? What was I supposed to do with a dead husband anyway? We never covered anything like this is in home ec class.

I called my parents and arranged for the kids to stay for a few days until I resolved the dead Harold situation.

The next morning, I took Harold to our family doctor. The doctor fainted. After all he had signed the death certificate. To his credit, after he was revived, he popped a couple of pills and behaved very professionally. He examined and questioned Harold, all the time casting glances at me as if I would suddenly say "April Fools." After checking him over, with a straight face he said "He's definitely dead. It's too bad because he's such a…"

"Yeah, yeah such a "nice guy" I interrupted. "Tell me something I don't already know, you quack." I cradled my head in my hands. "I'm so sorry. I didn't mean that. My nerves have been a bit frayed lately."

I never really noticed it before, but have men always been so clueless and utterly useless or is it just me?

I am not heartless. I am not without feelings and understanding. I couldn't just turn him out into the streets, not with him being dead and all. Where would he go? Would he camp out at the cemetery? Loiter around at the funeral home? Haunt an old house like a ghost? No, I couldn't let that happen. He is Harold. My Harold. We fixed up the garage and he stays there in his own sanctuary. The kids, God bless them, nothing seems to faze them. They have adapted and seem to love him even more than ever. The dog does too, but the cat won't go anywhere near him. This is a strange twist in our little tale, but at least he didn't come back all evil and decaying wanting to eat our brains. He doesn't cause any problems. He doesn't cost anything. He just sits in the garage with the dog waiting for the kids to come home from school. Harold's a wonderful house sitter. No one would dare break into a house with a dead watchman. The downside is none of our friends will visit. He doesn't have any strange habits, other than the being dead thing, and he does whatever you ask him to do with no arguments.

All in all, having a dead husband isn't what I would have wanted, but it's not so bad. I guess we are still married. I'll have to check into that. After all I wouldn't want to be living in sin with a dead man. But, he is Harold, and how can you say no to such "a nice guy."

FROZEN END

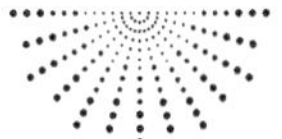

Like rush hour traffic, all my forward momentum had to come to an irritating stop. Any noise, movement, or random thought was enough of a distraction to gain the eager cooperation of my delinquent attention. Concentration had left my universe of abilities. I would stare at the stark white screen of my computer all day and return to the same blank screen the next day. I would show up every day, but I was like a fish with no fins; I couldn't swim. I knew I was in real trouble when the book stopped being my baby and became my adversary. I needed to take drastic actions, or I was never going to never give birth to this thing. I'd be book pregnant for a year and a half. I decided to take Mike's offer to use his cabin and hunker down in isolation to finish this task.

The cabin is located in the upper half of the Lower Peninsula of Michigan, on the eastern edge of the Manistee National Forest. It's near the tip of the little finger on the mitten; Michigan being shaped like one. It's a heavily forested and secluded area where peace and quiet are all you're going to get. Top that off with a typical brutal Michigan winter and its's solitary confinement. I'd finish this novel because there would simply be nothing else to do, a side from counting snowflakes.

I left Detroit on a Greyhound bus and went up the day after the new year. It had snowed only a little. The worst of the winter was yet to come, so travel was still doable. After reaching the town of Manistee, I paid the guy at the Mobil station with the massive Ford 350 to haul me and my gear up to the cabin. I'd purchased supplies for 4 months, even though I only planned to be there for 3. Mike kept the place stocked and in good condition, so my supplies were redundant, but I felt obligated.

"I hope you know that once you're there, it's for the duration. It gets pretty harsh up here this time of year. You'll be snowed in. The cabin is in a particularly rural area. The roads become impassable. You can't run down to the corner store for a six pack. There will be no one and nothing to help you till the thaw," the gas station owner said, assessing me with a sideward glance and finding me lacking.

"Don't worry about me. I'll be fine. I've been here before; granted only in the summer, but I know what to do." He let the matter drop with a disapproving raise of his doubting brow. I could hear him thinking. *"Smart-ass city boy. He ain't got a clue."*

The cabin was a rectangle building made of halved trees. A genuine log cabin complete with deer antler accessories, a root cellar, and a bear-skinned rug. It measured about 20 by 20 with a closet sized room added on the back as a bathroom. I'm being generous when I call it a bathroom. It was more of an attached outhouse. There's no bath. You have to empty the bucket after each use into the real outhouse 40 yards from the cabin. It was built because in the winter you couldn't easily get to the real outhouse. Thank God for sawdust. I couldn't complain, after all I got the place for free.

The cabin has two double paned windows. One on the south wall, one on the east wall, with the door on the north wall. There's a generous stone fireplace, a pump-handled sink, a beer cooler-sized ice chest, a sofa bed against the only unbroken wall, an easy chair. and a wobbly table with three equally wobbly chairs. Just the bare necessities.

Mike keeps the cabin for hunting, though he hadn't hunted in years. We would come up, a couple of times a year, for cards and beer during the milder seasons. He paid some people to keep an eye on it during the year but, it appeared they've been keeping a long distant eye on it because the place was coated in dust and spider webs. I was at it all day cleaning up, starting a fire, and settling myself in.

The first few days went as expected. The snowflakes arrived and brought lots of friends. It snowed and snowed and then it snowed some more. I was able to keep a good fire going. There was a winter's supply of chopped wood out back under the over-hang. I wouldn't have to split any unless I felt the urge to play at being a woodchuck. The generator was gassed up and ready to go, just in case. As well, there was a gas tank in the shed out back that would give me enough gas for a couple of months of generated power, if needed. Even though I purposely left behind all my elec-tronics, I brought my computer only because I needed it for writ-ing. With no telephone, no internet connection, no cable, or communication towers I was, "off the grid," as they say.

The only sounds in my fortress of solitude were the cracking of the fire and the turbulent winds that whipped up and tore down the snow drifts around the cabin. It whistled through the trees, rattled the windows, and now and then sent a cold gush down the chimney that excited the embers and produced a haze of smoke and ash in the room. Occasionally a passing deer would look in through the window and give me a, "who the hell are you?" look, then casually wander off. Or a flock of birds would land on the roof, stomp around the chimney to warm their feet, and take off again. The hoots of owls in search of a midnight snack were my only other visitors. At night there would be the distant howls of coyotes. It could have been the howl of dogs or wolves. How could my city boy ears tell the difference? I was just glad they never sounded too near.

It's amazing how much you can hear when the everyday

noises aren't there anymore. I relished the emptiness and fell into the peace of myself. It was nice to just be. I took long walks in the snow and sat in the cold air for hours. It was days, maybe weeks before I realized I hadn't spoken to anyone or made a sound. I began to pay attention to the sound of my breathing. My lungs taking in and releasing the clean, frigid air. It was musical and calming. I could have danced to the beat of my thumping heart, ever so regular and reassuring. It was like the percussions in a band keeping the tempo for my song. Even the stillness of my mind, as I thought of nothing for the first time in a very long time, was part of the melody I heard. The clearness of my thoughts was a revelation to me. I believed this was the best idea I had in years.

I stood on the edge of the cliff near the house, a sheer drop of 150 feet to the valley floor. It was a vertical wall of ice and snow. The panoramic view gave me perspective and a sense of clarity. With a clear head, I napped, thought, and contemplated all day. At night I would write. The words came to me in a flood, pouring themselves onto the pages like water from a pitcher. They were lyrical, as if my characters were singing their parts.

The joy and not just the job of writing came back to me. It got so good I felt that I was not writing a book, but channeling it. The characters took over and I just wrote down what they said and did. I became the audience and the chronicler. After a month, I was done with the first draft and in total edit mode.

One day about seven weeks into my stay, I had the strangest feeling. I was out walking when a strange feeling overcame me. A shiver went down my spine. I felt I would come apart and shatter to the wind. I held myself together only because I was willing it that way. The individual parts of me seem to belong somewhere else. Every inch of me had its own mind; its own life. I panted my way through it and eventually shook the feeling but, it troubled me all day. If I got sick there was no way to get help.

The weather grew increasingly colder. I kept a roaring blaze going day and night. One night I noticed I had trouble striking the A key on the type writer. Looking at my hand I was startled to realize I had no little finger on my left hand. I stopped shocked at this revelation. I could not remember when and how I had lost that finger. The night was lost to my studying my hand and searching for the lost memory.

The next morning after breakfast I brought in more wood and got a splinter in my right palm. I removed my gloves and began extracting the splinter. I froze in horror as I saw my left hand was missing not only my little finger but, my ring finger, as well.

"What the hell!" I shouted. I examined the hand and just like the night before the fingers seem to have never been there. The skin was smooth and seamless. There was no pain and no memory. It did not feel odd or wrong that they were gone, only surprising. I paced around the cabin, stopping, looking at my hand and returning to pacing.

"What is going on? How the hell can you lose three fingers and not remember it? Was I born like this and can't remember? Was this how I grew up so to me it was normal? If that's the case, why can't I remember? "I walked myself to sleep still hunting for answers. I woke with my hand in a fist pressed to my heart. I looked down at a hand with only a thumb. Panic took over. "Oh God. What is happening? Am I losing my mind? Have I lost my mind?"

I ran to the door threw it open and looked at the massive mountains of snow. The cold wind slapped me in the face and pushed me back into the room. Another shutter went down my spine. I realized that leaving was the one thing I couldn't do. I shut the door and sat dumbstruck on the sofa. I didn't sleep for days afraid that if I did, I didn't know what I would wake up to.

I would reluctantly doze off or look away and some part of me would be gone. First the rest of my fingers, then my toes disappeared; one by one. Eventually my hands, my arms, my feet, my calves and on up until my thighs deserted me. The insanity of seeing my body dissolve away drove me to fits of crying, screaming, and hours of cursing, praying, and more hours of psychotic laughter. I was trapped, helpless, and disappearing right before my eyes.

Wild fantasies ran through my mind. I thought demons were

eating me piece by piece every time I dozed off. I imagined that aliens were dissecting me as some experiment on human anatomy. Or maybe there was a mad man out there who was sneaking in when I slept and cutting me up for laughs. I thought that maybe I had multiple personalities and one of them was taking over and cutting me into pieces. In some bizarre way I was my own psycho killer. Then, just maybe, none of this was really happening and I was stuck in a nightmare, or a patient in a mental institution, or a schizo off his meds.

I'm not sure, but I vaguely remember being a limbless body with a head propped up on the sofa babbling incoherently. My body faded away inch by inch until I was a disembodied head perched on the sofa like some nightmarish jack-o-lantern. Or maybe I just ended.

Weeks later, during the spring thaw, a body was found at the base of the cliff wall. It was frozen solid and missing a pinky finger. Beside the body was a copy of a manuscript, titled "Frozen End".

TWO, FOUR, SIX

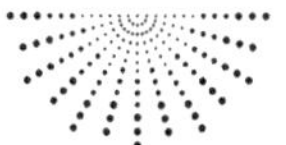

Alex and Carl crept through the thick haze. Feeling their way more than seeing. The thick mix of dust and fog coated the air like paint on a wall. Crawling under twisted grating they descended into the murky hollow of a collapsed building, escaping one devastation for another. Forcing a path between, over, and under the mountainous pile of rubbish, they made their way down. Large compound eyes used to sparse light guided them forward as they scurried through the near total darkness. Deep in the shrouded cavern they leveled off.

"There it is," Carl said. "It must have been hiding down here. You know… after… the thing."

"Yeah, the thing," said Alex. The thought caused a shutter to run through his body. His wings fluttered sending added dust into the air.

"The scent is sure to draw others."

"Though we haven't seen anyone else, I'm sure they're out there," replied Alex. "We're lucky to be the first to find this one. In a little while there won't be any of it left." Alex stared at the dried blood and stiffened limbs of their new found treasure and lowered his antennae giving a salute of thanks. "I wonder if there are any more of them left alive."

"Somewhere no doubt. They can't all be dead," Carl answered in a disappointed tone.

Diffused light penetrated down through cracks in the debris, creating a shadowy backdrop to the carnage surrounding them. Rancid dark ooze dripped down on the tons of scattered waste collecting into small black pools, as if the building was weeping dark tears over its destruction. Cool winds squeezed through the ragged labyrinth like air through a straw. The gust swirled about lifting thick layers of dirt that coated, rose to uncovered and settled again to recoat everything.

"It's amazing how little there is left. The destruction was so complete. They really did it this time," Alex scanned the shattered concrete, splintered wood, twisted metal and sighed.

"I'm just surprised it took them so long," Carl said, his antennae bending in the breeze. "If they had one talent, it was for making bigger and better messes. You've heard the stories. You know about the wars and their cavalier attitude toward life; even their own. The way they acted as if everything was made just for them and nobody else. My family had to move further and further away to stay safe until there was barely any place left to go."

"I know," Alex replied. "We ran too. I'm still worried about the effects it's had on my young ones."

"You would think that something so big wouldn't be so…so stupid. It was bad enough they never cared about what they were doing to the world. Or to the other creatures in it. As if the world isn't big enough for all of us. If you weren't like them, they would just as soon kill you. How many died from just their carelessness? If they hadn't wiped each other out, they very well might have wiped us all out." Carl said, standing on four legs poking their find with the other two.

"That's defeatist thinking," came a booming voice from the darkness. Alex and Carl looked up to see Bob descending the mountain of rubble. "They considered themselves superior to everything else. They felt entitled. It was their mission to make the world as they saw fit for them, regardless of how it affected any other creature. They were self-centered, self-important vermin. Worse than vermin, they were parasites, greedy and arrogant. They are an affliction. I say good riddance. The world will be a better place without them. I hope every last one of them is dead and gone." Bob stopped at the base of the rock pile. He unfurled his translucent wings and shook himself throwing off a cloud of dust.

"They couldn't have meant for it to turn out like this, Bob" said Alex, wiping film from his eyes. "After all, I don't think they meant to kill themselves. They proved not to be so clever, but they weren't bent on their own destruction."

"H!," he snapped, wiping ooze from a back leg flicking it away. "It's no wonder they did themselves in. Have you ever taken a serious look at them? The way they lived? They would mix together. Inter-bred and cohabitate. All types, all kinds, all colors. Like hungry maggots. No regard for the purity of the species. No concern for the natural order of things. Breeding like rain drops in a thunderstorm, soiling everything they touched. You'd never see us do that. We respect order. We understand that everything and everyone has their place." He rose up elongating his body, twitched his mandibles, and spit out a wad of dirt and saliva.

"They subjugate everything, even their own kind, wreaking havoc, using up the world until there hardly was one. It was only a matter of time before we came to this." He swept the air with all three right legs balancing on the other three. "The superior species, my ass. Look around you. This is what their superiority brings." He growled out the last words turning in a circle frowning at the scene.

"I'm afraid he's right," said Carl. "It's all their fault. I think the world will be a better place without them. If they stayed around I think we would have had to go to war. Sooner or later."

"Sooner I say," shouted Bob.

"War," Alex replied. "That's crazy. We aren't violent. What do we know of war? We've always been about survival. I heard those rumors, but I always thought it was just ego talking. Could we have ever hoped to win a war against them? I mean, they're so big and they have machines and things."

"Yes, we could." Declared Bob proudly. "We have numbers on our side. There are billions upon billions of us in the world. If we ban together nothing could stand in our way. For some time, there has been talk of war. Even the rats agreed, and you know what unpleasant, deceitful, and vile creatures they are." He lowered his body and spread his antennae wide to draw them in.

"Mark my words, one day we'll have to deal with them. If we don't, it will be the same thing all over again. They'll try to dominate, just like the two legs did. Rats are untrustworthy and malicious. Can you imagine rats running things? Never! It doesn't matter if they have two legs or four legs they're all the same."

"*Or six legs*," Alex thought. He twitched his mandibles and gave Bob a sideward glance.

"Everybody," Bob continued. "Every species was in agreement except the termites. They are, as always, a single minded and uncooperative clan. They just built their tunnels deeper and said they would go it alone. What do you expect from a bunch of eunuchs led by a female? But, the rest of us saw the necessity of stopping those towering menaces."

Bob marched around a pool of ooze. "They hunted, starved, and poisoned off the large beast. Killing most for the fun of it. The others fell to their fancies and industries. The talk got serious when the frogs and fishes died out. The waters had become so foul they just couldn't survive in it. When the creatures of the sky, all but disappeared because the air was so thick with their waste, the talk turned desperate. Desperation turned to anger and anger to action." He stomped his feet in exhilaration.

Bob's big black eyes gleamed as his pace quickened and his volume grew. Striking out, he kicked a tiny stone from his path delighting in the physical exertion. Alex drew back and lowered himself. Carl stood transfixed flexing each individual segment of his antennae not sure how to react.

"We were determined not to allow the land to become as barren and lifeless as the oceans. Coalitions started forming.

Armies were beginning to amass. But, wouldn't you know it?" He stopped, angled his head, and looked at them as if he had just noticed they were there. "Before we could act, they went and did it. The fools, the dam witless idiots went and killed themselves; almost taking us and the rest of the world with them. Huh. It would be funny if we weren't living the consequences."

Carl circled around the dead thing, extended one antennae to touch it and ripped off a piece with his mandibles. With a large chunk torn from the carcass he said, "you do realize that all of them probably aren't dead, don't you?"

"None of them could have survived. I don't believe it. Look at this one. It lasted for a few days, but they all must be like this by now." said Alex.

"I have to agree with him," said Bob, pointing his antennas at Carl like a judge picking the winner. "They are a hardy bunch, not easy to get rid of. You would have to be to live the way they did. Don't think we have given up. The ants, the beetles, the worms and other things that live underground have spread out to hunt them down. We will search the whole world. When we find them in their hiding places we will deal with them, permanently. They are too dangerous. There is no living together. It's us or them." He dry-washed his front legs. "We are going to take back the world and this time we'll come out on top."

Alex bristled at the thought. He moved to gather his share of the harvest. "We, you keep saying we. I don't want war. Look outside. Look around you. Hasn't there been enough destruction and death? We need to concentrate on survival, not war. We have families." He widened his eyes refracting the dim light. "There already isn't enough to eat. The air is so thick you can't see through it. All you can smell and taste is ashes. The ground is dry and cracked and what water you can find is just puddles of ooze like those over there." He pointed to one of the black puddles. "So, don't give me talk of war. We need time to recover from this."

Breaking the tension, Carl said. "The world will eventually

heal itself, Alex. I think. The sky will clear up and the plants will start to grow again. We just have to hold out until then, that's all."

Alex extended an antenna to his companion. "I don't know, Carl. We traveled a long way to find this. How long can we hold out before there's nothing left? In the meantime they're planning more of this," he angled one antennae at Bob and the other at the broken landscape.

Bob pulled his antennae back against his body and stood motionless as if the statements shocked him. "Times will be difficult," he said, resuming his pacing. "But we will survive. We always survive. We have been here for almost as long as there has been a world. We will be here as long as there is one. We are survivors."

"Even if we do survive, what kind of a world are we talking about? All I've heard you say is war this and destroy that. Is it worthwhile if we build the same world we're complaining about?" Alex asked, rocking from side to side.

"We won't make the same mistakes they did. Our world would be better. You'll see," offered Carl. "Besides there's not…"

"Don't think like that. We're not like them. We're better than them," interrupted Bob pointing his antennae at the dead thing. "We know what we're doing. If you are on our side you will see. We'll do it right. Never again scurrying out of the way of the powerful or hiding in the shadows. We won't be the soil under anyone's feet. Now we will be the feet to be avoided." Bob marched in place stomping the ground.

Twisting his antennas together, Alex gathered his stash and started toward the climb. "I've got to get back Carl. The others will be waiting. You coming?"

Carl gathered his share and followed. Near the exit they turned to look at Bob. He was standing upright on his hind legs, the other four legs spread wide, his antennae dueling with each other. "We claim dominion. The world is ours now," he shouted.

Out in the dim, against the dust and wind, Alex turned to Carl. "Does it just start all over again?"

"Did it ever really stop?" came the reply.

ABOUT THE AUTHOR

F.R. Wilson is a retired electrician who is now fulfilling his lifelong dream of publishing all of the books he's wanted to write. *Small Bites* is his fifth fantasy novel.

 facebook.com/franklin.wilson.31

www.ingramcontent.com/pod-product-compliance
Lightning Source LLC
Chambersburg PA
CBHW072303130726
47910CB00012B/2422